A dull roaring
sounds aroun
of her heart fe
thundering inside her body as
Anika stared at him.

"What?" She finally managed to gasp.

"You want me. I want you."

"I never said I wanted you," she sputtered.

Nicholas watched her, his fingers pressing more firmly against her back, his eyes glowing with that same predatory light she'd glimpsed on the catamaran.

"You also never said you didn't. So tell me now, Anika. Tell me you haven't thought about me kissing you. Tell me," he continued, his husky voice washing over her and sending sinful shivers racing over her body, "you didn't think about how we'd be together when you were in my arms on the boat. That you didn't imagine me tracing my fingers, my lips, over every inch of your incredible body."

Say something!

But she couldn't. Not when her imagination was conjuring up carnal images of her and Nicholas entwined, arms wrapped around each other as he trailed his lips over her neck, her breasts, his hips pressing against hers without any barriers between them.

"Ah." His smile deepened. "So you have thought about it."

Hot Winter Escapes

Sun, snow and sexy seductions...

Whether it's a trip to the Swiss Alps or a rendezvous on a gorgeous Hawaiian beach, warming up in front of the fire or basking in the sizzling sun, these billion-dollar getaways provide the perfect backdrops for even more scorching winter romances and passionately-ever-afters!

Escape to some winter sun in...

Bound by Her Baby Revelation by Cathy Williams

An Heir Made in Hawaii by Emmy Grayson

Claimed by the Crown Prince by Abby Green

One Forbidden Night in Paradise by Louise Fuller

And get cozy in these luxurious snowy hideaways...

A Nine-Month Deal with Her Husband
by Joss Wood

Snowbound with the Irresistible Sicilian
by Maya Blake

Undoing His Innocent Enemy
by Heidi Rice

In Bed with Her Billionaire Bodyguard
by Pippa Roscoe

All available now!

Emmy Grayson

AN HEIR MADE IN HAWAII

ISBN-13: 978-1-335-59215-6

An Heir Made in Hawaii

Copyright © 2023 by Emmy Grayson

For questions and comments about the quality of this book, please contact us at CustomerService@Harlequin.com.

Harlequin Enterprises ULC
22 Adelaide St. West, 41st Floor
Toronto, Ontario M5H 4E3, Canada
www.Harlequin.com

Printed in U.S.A.

Emmy Grayson wrote her first book at the age of seven about a spooky ghost. Her passion for romance novels began a few years later with the discovery of a worn copy of Kathleen Woodiwiss's *A Rose in Winter* buried on her mother's bookshelf. She lives in the Midwest countryside with her husband (who's also her ex-husband), their children and enough animals to start their own zoo.

Books by Emmy Grayson

Harlequin Presents

Cinderella Hired for His Revenge
His Assistant's New York Awakening

The Infamous Cabrera Brothers

His Billion-Dollar Takeover Temptation
Proof of Their One Hot Night
A Deal for the Tycoon's Diamonds

The Van Ambrose Royals

A Cinderella for the Prince's Revenge
The Prince's Pregnant Secretary

Visit the Author Profile page
at Harlequin.com.

To Mr. Grayson, always

To my favorite proofreading team, Mom and Dad

To one of my biggest cheerleaders, Little Man

To my Queen of One Lines, Katelyn

To my friend who is stronger than she knows, Laura

CHAPTER ONE

ANIKA PIERCE SAT back on her towel and gazed out over the pristine waters of Hanalei Bay. No one looking out over the calm, gentle waves would have guessed that just the night before the ocean had churned and frothed beneath the weight of a late-November storm. The heaviest rains of the season in the Hawaiian island usually didn't start until December. But the storm hadn't gotten the memo, barreling across the ocean and turning the midnight blue waves to black. She'd watched it from the hotel balcony, bewitched by the jagged bolts of lightning and the rumble of thunder that had made the windows tremble. The fierce beauty of it all had thrilled her, called to something primal deep inside.

Anika snorted. Or perhaps it had just been a perfect mirror of her mood. And all because of *him*.

Nicholas Andrew Lassard. The bastard.

She'd walked out onto the hotel's terrace that overlooked the waters of the Pacific Ocean just after breakfast this morning, soaking in everything from the soaring palm trees to the mountains that guarded the Hanalei Valley. She loved Slovenia and the small town of Bled that had become her home. But she was going to take full advantage of the summer-like weather. With a hot cup of tea in one hand and a book in the other, she'd been excited to lie out on one of the chaise lounges and enjoy her morning.

Until she'd turned and run smack into Nicholas. If there was one thing to take joy in, it was that her tea had ended up all over his crisp white shirt. He hadn't reacted with anger, even though the shirt probably cost as much as what she charged for a night at the inn. No, he'd simply smiled that charming Scottish smile and told her it was good to see her. Then, when she'd demanded to know what he was doing here, he'd calmly replied he was attending the International Hospitality & Tourism Conference.

Just thinking about the smug expression on his handsome face stoked the simmering embers of irritation into hot spurts of anger that roiled about in her chest. When he'd walked into the Zvonček Inn, three weeks ago with yet another offer to buy her hotel, this one with an increase of another hundred thousand euros compared to the offer he'd made over the summer, he'd seen the brochure for the conference on her desk. The arrogant jerk had even commented on it and asked if she was attending.

Had he followed her to Hawaii? Was he truly that fixated with buying the inn that he would fly nearly eight thousand miles and track her down?

Yes.

She had underestimated Nicholas when he'd swept into Bled a year and a half ago and begun construction on the Hotel Lassard at Lake Bled. A three-story luxury hotel with an on-site spa, restaurant and rooftop bar. Elegant, glamorous and ridiculously expensive.

And just down the road from the inn that had been in her mother's family since World War I.

The hotel had done their due diligence in sending a representative to meet with her and deliver a leather portfolio complete with architectural renderings of the future hotel. *"Community relations,"* the willow-thin girl in a fancy black suit had said with a huge smile that had reminded Anika of a shark. She hadn't been a fan of having another hotel so close to hers, especially one with all the modern amenities hers didn't have. But the kind of people who stayed at the Hotel Lassard were most definitely not the kind of people who stayed at the Zvonček

Inn. They wanted marble bathtubs and grand chandeliers, not cozy fireplaces and handmade quilts.

She'd met Nicholas a week later at a breakfast hosted by the local tourism board. With thick, dark brown hair that looked artlessly windblown and an actual dimple in his cheek when he smiled, he'd had half the women of Bled in love with him before they'd sat down. Irena, an elderly shopkeeper with huge round glasses perched on her nose, had breathlessly whispered the silver watch had to be Cartier and the charcoal-gray suit tailored to Nicholas's broad shoulders and lean waist was most definitely from Savile Row in London.

"See how perfectly it fits his rear?"

The memory of Irena's croaky voice teased a reluctant smile from her lips. Yes, Nicholas was a good-looking man. She could even acknowledge handsome. Too bad his greedy soul was so ugly.

The wealth, the charm, all of it had put her on guard. Nicholas walked in far different circles than she did. That he hadn't bothered to come and deliver the news of his new hotel to her in person had shown her that Nicholas took care of the big, flashy things, whereas little people such as herself were fobbed off onto his underlings. Seeing him flirt with women of all ages at the breakfast before he'd delivered a slick presentation on what his hotel would bring to the community had cemented her impression of an overindulged lothario who liked playing at the hotel business.

Except, when Nicholas wanted something, he played hardball. She'd found that out the hard way this past spring when he'd surprised her by walking into the inn and requesting a private meeting. His sheer presence, from another one of those custom suits down to his shiny loafers, had grated on her nerves and made the worn rug in her office and the pots of snowdrops on the windowsill feel meager and outdated.

He'd smiled at her. She'd given him the tiniest one in return.

And then he'd robbed her of speech by sliding another leather portfolio with the embossed silver logo of the Hotel Lassard onto her desk, one with an offer to buy the inn for fifty thousand euros above its current value.

He'd taken advantage of her silence. His words had flowed out, smooth as brandy and just as potent, with that charming accent underlying his pitch.

He'd been satisfied, he'd said, with the property they'd purchased and its views of not only the lake but the island and its romantic church, the castle on the northwestern shore. Yet the one thing he hadn't gotten was lakeside property. He'd accepted it, he'd said with all the humbleness of spoiled royalty, content to have the views.

Until he'd taken a tour of the lake and seen her inn from the water. He'd even used the Slovenian term, *pletna*, for the gondola-like boats that ferried tourists around, smiling slightly as if he was proud of himself for bothering to use the word correctly.

Her inn, he'd explained, could be a perfect extension of the Hotel Lassard. With extensive renovating, the integrity of the building could be kept while adding the luxury and glamour that guests of the Lassard brand expected. It would also give his clients access to the small beach for swimming and lounging in the summer, as well as the dock for year-round boat launches.

Then he'd leaned forward and said the words that even now made her grate her teeth just remembering how self-righteous he'd sounded.

"I know the inn is in trouble. I can fix it."

To his credit, he'd only blinked when she'd said, "No." He'd leaned back, his chair creaking ominously. For once, she'd wished something in the inn would break and send him tumbling to the floor.

He'd asked why. She'd replied the inn wasn't

for sale. He'd added one hundred thousand euros to the offer on the spot.

And damn it, she'd been tempted. For one horrible second, she'd been tempted. Yes, the inn was aging. It seemed like every time she turned around, mattresses were needing to be replaced, a window had to be repaired or one of the ancient water boilers was on the verge of dying. Decisions that had fallen to her more and more as her grandmother, Marija, had grown sick. Decisions that tangled with worry about her grandmother and weighed on her so heavily that some nights she would lie in bed and feel like she could barely catch her breath wondering how she would possibly overcome it all.

Accepting Nicholas's offer would have been the easy way out. The inn had been in her family for over a hundred years. Walking the halls where her mother, Danica, had grown up, reading on the same window seat and walking barefoot in the yard in the spring when the snowdrops the inn had been named for covered the ground in a blanket of white blooms, had been a lifeline she'd desperately needed. After Danica had passed, Anika had journeyed from the States to live with her only remaining family. Marija, and the inn, had saved her.

But it wasn't just her family or their legacy on the line. The guests who came back year after year considered the inn a home away from home. She wasn't going to let some arrogant hotel scion turn it into a ritzy getaway her clients would no longer be able to afford, to turn her inheritance into a splashy spectacle. All because the bastard wasn't satisfied with his views of the lake.

She'd said no again. The smile had disappeared, giving her a glimpse of what Nicholas Lassard concealed so well behind that pleasant face: a sharp, intelligent businessman who didn't like being denied what he wanted.

No. She was not letting him ruin something else on this trip. She was here for the conference. Hopefully she would pick up some ideas and make some contacts that would bring more business. But she was also heeding the advice Marija had bestowed on her that final week before she'd passed when she'd given Anika an envelope containing a plane ticket and a reservation for the conference they'd always dreamed of one day attending together.

"Go and enjoy yourself." She'd squeezed Anika's hand when Anika opened her mouth to protest, to point out the money would have been better spent on the inn. *"Do it for me, Anika. I'll be happier knowing you have a chance to live a little."*

The concrete dock jutted out into the water

and offered the most incredible views. The end was covered by a canopy and offered several picnic tables as well as ladders for those wanting to swim off the pier. But at eight o'clock in the morning, the pier was blissfully empty.

Sailboats and a couple smaller fishing boats gently bobbed on the water. Tourists in kayaks paddled across the bay and into the Hanalei River. Beyond the water and the beach, mountains swelled up toward the sky, the jagged ridges hinting at the wildness beyond.

She missed home, missed the crispness of fall sliding into winter as snow danced down from the Alps and dusted the town and the adjoining lake. Lake Bled was becoming better known as a travel destination, although it had held on to its small-town European charm.

But Hawaii had rekindled a wanderlust she hadn't felt in years. She hadn't even known she'd needed to get away from Slovenia until she had stepped out of Kauai's airport into tropical heat that had slid across her skin like a lover's caress. Palm trees had provided shade, mountains covered in velvety green instead of snow had stood proudly against a turquoise sky and, perhaps her favorite part of all, were the chickens that had run about with carefree glee.

Determined to relax before she walked back up for the conference's opening session, she lay back on her towel. Slowly, she focused on relaxing her body, tension seeping out of her muscles as the sun gently wiped away her worries and lulled her into a dreamlike state. Schedules and overdue bills and marketing plans slipped away. For once her mind was completely, blissfully clear of everything except where she was.

The word drifted through her mind again—*heaven*—and she let out a sigh of contentment.

"Be a shame to burn that beautiful skin."

She froze as the deep, gravelly voice rolled over her, each of the words pronounced with emphasis and tinted with his rasping accent. The rigidity returned, invading her body and tensing her limbs into tightly coiled springs as her pulse kicked up a notch.

Because he's annoying as hell, she reassured herself.

A shadow fell over her, blocking the sun. Reluctantly, she opened her eyes and blinked.

"I was wrong."

Nicholas loomed over her, white smile flashing against tan skin that said he had recently been traveling, or more likely partying, abroad.

"About what?"

"I'm not in heaven. I'm in hell."

He threw back his head and laughed. She propped herself up on her elbows and glared up at him, trying to contain the burst of fury that raced through her. Normally Nicholas only inspired minor irritation, occasionally a dash of righteous anger.

But right now, when she had just achieved the peak of relaxation, she wanted nothing more than to shove him off the pier.

"It'll be hot enough this afternoon to count as hell."

"What are you doing here?"

He arched a brow as he crouched down next to her.

"Same as you."

"Trying to have some alone time?"

"Yes."

Her hands curled into fists. "The definition of alone means no one else around."

He glanced around the bay in a slow, considering manner that made her want to grind her teeth.

"Hmm. Must have missed the sign that said this was a private pier."

He pulled his sunglasses off as he spoke. A different type of heat rolled over her, swift and so shocking it made her lips part in surprise. She'd never had a physical reaction to him before. Maybe it was his proximity. Perhaps it was the woodsy scent of his aftershave winding around her.

Or you just haven't been on a date in forever.

Latching on to that rational excuse, she channeled the unexpected jolt into the glare she slanted at him. He arched an amused brow. The chiseled planes of his angular face and defined jawline made the contrast of deep blue eyes that always seemed to glint with amusement all the more alluring.

He's the enemy! her brain screamed. *Stop fantasizing!*

"Cut the crap, Nick. Why are you here?"

His grin flashed once again, confident and sexy. "I like that you still hold on to your American phrases."

"And I like you when you're not around."

"You wound me, Anika. We're not only colleagues but neighbors. Shouldn't we at least act hospitable to one another?"

"I'll acknowledge that we are, unfortunately, neighbors," Anika replied. "However, *colleagues* would imply we both work for a living. I work, whereas you splash your face on magazines and reap the money of the hard work done by your employees as you plot how to take over small businesses like mine and add to your treasury. So I think *colleagues* is a bit too generous a term."

His smirk spread into a smile. She blinked, uncomfortable with the heat flickering low in her belly. Yes, the man was handsome. But he was also a pampered, sneaky snake.

"This is fun. We should talk more."

"I'm insulting you, not conversing."

"Still, one of the more enjoyable conversations I've had in ages."

"Did you follow me here?" she asked, trying to get him back on track.

"I was invited to be a guest speaker for one of the conference's panels in the spring. I've been slated to speak for months."

"You might have mentioned that when I told you I was going," she snapped.

"And risk you canceling? I couldn't have that, especially," he added as his voice deepened, "as this might just be the thing to bring us together."

Alarm skittered through her. "There's no 'us,' Nick. Never is, never will be."

His smile didn't falter even as his gaze sharpened, intense and suddenly focused on what he wanted. There was the heir apparent to his father's hotel empire, the man who would stop at nothing to get what he wanted. The next time he'd visited the inn, a bigger offer in hand, he'd stood in her lobby like he already owned it. When she'd ordered him to leave, he'd listed all the repairs she was facing down, a list that had made her inwardly wince as he included the estimated costs for each repair. Yet it had also reinforced her resolve that he was the last person on the earth she wanted to hand over the inn to. That he had violated her privacy to such an extent, dug so deeply into her personal finances to acquire his own goals, had driven her to slide the offer out of the folder, hold it up and rip it down the middle right in front of his eyes.

He'd been back. Oh, he'd been back repeatedly through the summer, each offer more than the last.

Which made her all the more determined to keep his greedy hands off her family's inn.

"Why do you resist? My offer could do nothing but help you."

"I think you mean ruin," she shot back, hating that his tone stayed so calm and collected while hers vibrated with indignation. "With how much you're always off gallivanting around the world—"

"Miss me, Pierce?"

His hand came up and brushed a stray tendril of hair back from her face. Something crossed his face, something that made her stomach flutter.

Then it was gone, so quickly she wondered if she'd imagined it.

Get a grip.

Her reaction to Nicholas was simple biology. Whether she liked it or not, he was attractive.

She hadn't dated anyone in nearly two years, and the couple of times she and Zachary had attempted sex, it had been less than satisfying.

Don't think about sex! Not around him.

"I miss the solitude and peace I enjoy when you're not around. Now go away, let me enjoy my morning and," she added sharply, "keep your fancy manicured hands off my property."

He reached down and, before she could pull away, threaded his fingers through hers and held up her hand. Their palms met, pressed together in an intimate caress that swept through with a fiery intensity. It took a moment for the reality of his calloused skin to penetrate her shock.

"I've never gotten a manicure."

His voice slid over her, his tone deeper, sultry like the warmth slowly building as the sun climbed higher in the sky. She should pull her hand away. But as his fingers drifted down, traced the lines crisscrossing her palm, then lower to settle on the pulse beating wildly in her wrist, she didn't move. When his gaze returned to her face, she couldn't stop her sharp intake of breath as she saw something she'd never expected to see in Nicholas's eyes.

Desire.

A memory of the last tabloid image she'd seen appeared in her mind. He'd been looking at his now ex-girlfriend with the same focused intensity, one hand resting casually around her waist as she'd smiled up at him on the rooftop of some famous museum.

Nicholas Lassard wasn't made for family, for commitment and wedding rings and babies. She wanted all of it. What she didn't want was to be the latest in a long string of conquests.

The thought gave her enough willpower to pull her hand away. She turned away from him, her eyes seeking out the palm trees swaying gently in the breeze. She breathed in deeply and refocused on the issue at hand.

Something needed to be done. She knew it, had known it as she'd arranged for the necessary repairs to the structure of the inn when paint had begun to peel and the carpets had become more worn.

Selling the inn might save her financially. But it would be saying goodbye to a legacy, watching it turn from a cozy haven into a swanky offshoot of a hotel that offered champagne in crystal flutes at check-in and heated outdoor pools. The essence of the Zvonček Inn would be lost.

As would the only thing she had left of her family.

"You run a resort that costs over a thousand dollars a night and twenty-four-seven room service. I work in an inn that uses antique keys."

She glanced at his black T-shirt and linen pants. Even at the beach, his wardrobe screamed wealth.

"We run in very different circles. You stick to yours and stay out of my way, I'll stick to mine, and everyone stays happy."

His hand settled on her calf. She jerked at the feel of his bare palm on her skin, then inwardly cursed for reacting to his touch.

"Does it make you happier to be away from me, Anika?"

"Yes."

"I'm wounded."

Frustrated, she stood, so swiftly she nearly knocked Nicholas back on his rear. Satisfied in the most petulant way possible, she turned her back on him and whisked her dress over her head. A strangled noise made her look back over her shoulder.

Nicholas was staring at her. Was *stare* even the right word, she thought frantically as he rose, his eyes raking her body.

"What are you doing?"

"Going for a swim."

"Don't be a fool," he growled. "There's high surf in the winter and—"

"And a smart tourist just might ask the lifeguards over at the beach if today was safe for swimming before she went in," she snapped back. It was much easier to ignore the fire and possession in his gaze when he acted like a macho idiot. "Don't underestimate me, Nicholas. You'll lose."

With those parting words, she jumped off the pier into the waters of Hanalei Bay.

CHAPTER TWO

NICHOLAS ACCEPTED THE pen from the perky red-headed clerk behind the counter. He didn't miss the appreciation in her eyes, nor the brush of her fingers against his.

"We just need your signature here, here and here."

"Saying I won't sue if I get eaten by a turtle?"

The clerk chuckled. "To date, we've had no turtle attacks. Have you ever been on a turtle snorkeling tour, Mr. Lassard?"

"Snorkeling, yes, but not for turtles."

The woman's smile switched from flirty to genuine. "Then you're in for a treat. Their nesting season is from May to September, but we've had plenty of guests see them in the winter, too."

Nicholas returned her smile. "I'm looking forward to it."

"Do you think we'll see a dolphin, Mom?"

Nicholas glanced over to see a sandy-haired little boy excitedly tugging on his mother's shirt as they headed for the door. The woman smiled down at her son.

"I hope so."

"Or maybe a sea monster!"

Something in the boy's hopeful expression stabbed straight into Nicholas's gut. For a moment he saw David, sunny smile brightening his freckled face, his dark blond hair falling into his eyes because he'd refused to get it cut.

A smile extinguished in the span of a heartbeat by a careless driver who had missed a stop sign and changed his family's life forever.

His fingers tightened around the pen. He'd accepted, after years of counseling, that the driver had been at fault. An acceptance that had lessened, but not fully removed, the guilt that lingered beneath the surface. He'd been the one to suggest riding bikes that day, the one who had been looking the other way when David had ridden out into the road.

Behind him, he heard the door close and the sound of the little boy's chattering fade. The tightness in his chest eased a fraction. He finished scrawling his name.

"Thank you, Mr. Lassard." The clerk gestured towards a corner decorated with plush, vibrant blue chairs and a flat-screen TV mounted on the wall. "We have one more guest on the way. As soon as they arrive, I'll start the safety video."

He moved to a bank of windows that over-looked the harbor. He had been to Hawaii before with his parents, but they'd visited Maui on that trip. In the first ten years after David's death, the only time Nicholas and his parents had been happy was when they were on vacation. Thailand, Spain, Brazil, Alaska. They'd jetted all over the world, briefly escaping reality and indulging in adventure. As soon as they'd returned to their stately mansion in London overlooking Eaton Square gardens, his father had retreated to his office or flown off to take care of business somewhere else. His mother had crawled into bed and slept or taken pills to keep the grief at bay. They didn't talk about David. Unless they were on vacation, they'd barely talked at all.

He shoved his hands in his pockets and watched a family move toward the dock. This past summer had marked the twentieth anniversary of David's passing, and things had improved immensely in recent years. He didn't know what had finally driven his parents into counseling. But they'd recovered, slowly climbing out of their depression and rejoining life. It had been about that time that Nicholas approached his father about becoming more involved with the Hotel Lassard brand. His father had agreed with the stipulation that Nicholas work his way up. He'd started with a maintenance crew for the chain's flagship hotel in London on the weekends as he'd pursued his business degree at Oxford. He'd slowly but surely worked his way up to his current job as Director of Expansion.

Too bad that what had seemed like such a simple expansion, a way to achieve his vision for the Lake Bled hotel, had turned into such a chaotic mess.

Anika Pierce had caught his attention when he'd spoken to Bled's local business owners nearly eighteen months ago. Unlike the majority of attendees who had responded with wide-eyed excitement to his presentation, she'd been polite but chilly, asking intelligent questions that had heightened his interest. So had her overall professional appearance, from her dark hair caught up in a twist on the back of her head to her black trousers and a loose white shirt with a tie around her slender neck. But her frosty attitude had rankled. He'd ensured that representatives from the Hotel Lassard had connected with all of the local hotel owners in the area, to reassure them that he would be working with, not against, their interests. Perhaps Anika just didn't like having another hotel so close to her inn, even though his research and development team had assured him the inn and vacation rentals in the area were in an entirely different class than the Hotel Lassard.

Whatever the reason for Anika's snooty attitude, he was used to a different type of response from most women. Her lack of one, combined with the grudge she seemed to hold, had made it easy to not think of her when he'd left.

Business had taken him back to London, then New York and finally Bilbao in northern Spain. When he'd returned to Slovenia in the spring to see the construction, he'd taken the long route around the lake past the centuries-old castle that stood guard on the clifftops. He'd also booked himself a ride on one of the gondolas that frequented the lake's pristine waters. One of his father's most important lessons as Nicholas had ventured deeper into the family business had been to experience what his guests would as much as possible.

It had been on that boat ride, as the gondola circled the southern end of the island, that he'd looked toward the upper levels of the Hotel Lassard emerging above the treetops and seen the Zvonček Inn on the lakeshore. The simple beauty of it had hit him square in the chest, conjuring images of long-ago trips before David's passing, to destinations like the beaches of England and Ireland instead of cities bursting at the seams. In that moment, he'd had a clear vision of the future: the main hotel to the east, with an exclusive mansion for guests wanting more privacy or a room on the lake just a short walk away. The pier could be redone, with a terrace for dining and a dock for boat rides to the island. Luxury combined with the natural beauty Lake Bled offered.

When he'd toured his property in person, reviewed the aerial photos of the surrounding area, he hadn't even considered acquiring the inn. But once he'd seen it from the lake, nothing less than owning it would do. He hadn't analyzed the obsession that had suddenly seized him. Whatever was pushing him was pushing him in the right direction.

He'd gotten back in his car and turned at the wooden sign that advertised the Zvonček Inn. A small painting of the bell-shaped snowdrop flower the inn was named for had faded long ago, the white petals almost the same brown as the sign.

That had been his first clue of how the inn was doing. As he'd driven up the long drive, he'd given credit for whoever had planted the snowdrops blooming along the gravel, the simple charm further enhanced by the white lanterns marching up to the house.

The house itself had surprised him. Unlike the cottage style of so many buildings in the area, the three-story home reminded him more of Victorian-style houses he'd glimpsed on his trips to the Hamptons and Martha's Vineyard. From the tower topped with a conical roof to the expansive porch trimmed with intricate wood spirals that reminded him of a gingerbread house, it was the definition of quaint.

Or had been. Whatever pale color the house had once been painted had long since faded to gray. The porch sagged. Shingles were missing from the roof.

But there was promise. Nicholas had achieved far more with far less.

He'd anticipated Anika being a harder sell than most. But he never would have guessed she would be a flat-out denial. Not with the inn falling apart around her.

He'd considered approaching Marija Novack, Anika's grandmother. He'd met her a couple of times, including during the town's annual Winter Fairy Tale market, where she'd been manning a booth draped in evergreens and selling the inn's version of the traditional Bled cream cake. Aside from the tawny gold of her eyes, he hadn't glimpsed a single trace of Anika in the woman's deep smile or the feathery cap of silver hair on top of the narrow, slender face.

The sixth sense that had made him so successful, his ability to read people quickly and accurately, had noted the fatigue lurking in the crinkles by her eyes. The paleness of her skin. He might be resolute, tenacious, heavy-handed when the situation called for it. But he wasn't cruel. He wasn't going to press a woman who, at best, was getting on in years.

Unfortunately, his suspicions that something else was going on had been confirmed that summer. He'd backed off as Marija had neared the end of her life, had even sent flowers to her funeral and given Anika space to mourn her grandmother in private. He knew, better than most, how important it was to grieve. Especially when someone you loved so deeply was there one moment and then gone the next.

He turned away from the harbor and moved over to the table set up with fruit, coffee and *malasadas*, thick, chewy doughnuts that were a breakfast favorite in the islands. He poured himself a cup of black coffee, savored the underlying flavor of molasses and focused on the slight burning on his tongue from drinking it before it had a chance to cool.

Better to focus on that than the past.

Especially when the present, and more importantly the future, demanded so much of his attention.

Including one stubborn, infuriating inn owner.

He'd given her time, nearly three months after Marija's passing. But as the opening date of the Hotel Lassard had drawn nearer, he'd decided to press forward. When he'd heard that a tree had taken out the roof of one of the guest rooms during an autumn storm, he'd returned with an even higher offer and the opportunity for Anika to remain as the general manager of the property. It had been more than generous.

A view Anika had not shared, judging by how she'd ripped this one not down the middle but into long, thin strips she'd fed into the fireplace crackling in her office.

He'd been angry, yes. He wasn't used to hearing the word *no* and, as he'd discovered over the last few months, he didn't like it. Some might argue he had been indulged too often. But when it came to business, it had nothing to do with being spoiled and everything to do with the fact that not only was purchasing the inn the right move for his hotel, but it was the best thing for Anika before that damned house collapsed on top of her.

Stubborn, prideful woman.

Yet beneath his annoyance, something else had started to simmer, then pulse through his veins when she'd turned to face him, crossing her arms over her chest and arching one eyebrow with a smug smirk on her full lips.

Desire. It had unnerved him to the point that he had left Anika with the less than witty retort of "This isn't over" before he'd walked out, putting as much distance between him and her as possible.

He enjoyed women. Their beauty, their company, their beds. He wasn't like some of his class who took a new woman out every night or, worse, balanced multiple lovers at once. But he wasn't a saint, either. He had no intention of marrying, of having children. Not after seeing the devastation David's death had wrought on his parents' marriage, straining it to the breaking point far too many times. Yes, they'd survived and eventually found a new kind of happiness. But years of his mother drifting about the house, a medicated wraith, and his father traveling so much he barely saw his wife and surviving son, had been enough.

Toss in the guilt that had never relinquished its hold on him and he was left with a firm commitment to bachelorhood.

And something about Anika, his reaction to her, told him it wouldn't be straightforward and easy. No, Anika Pierce was a challenging woman with hidden depths and a fire that would ensnare him.

A point proven by the eye-popping sight he'd witnessed yesterday morning. When Anika had stood and stripped off her dress, he'd nearly swallowed his tongue. Beneath the loose shirts and wide-legged trousers she usually wore back in Slovenia was an incredible body shown off to perfection by a deep orange bikini. A body that had made him uncomfortably hard as he'd taken in the subtly defined back, trim waist and generous curves of her thighs. When she'd turned, hair the color of dark chocolate streaming over her shoulders and fire snapping in her golden brown eyes, he knew he was in trouble. He hadn't anticipated how much he wanted to touch that pale skin, slide his hands over her hips and pull her against his body and find out just how much passion Anika had been hiding under that cool exterior of hers.

As if to further torment him, her husky voice sounded behind him, low and pleasant. Surprised, he turned to see her smiling at the red-haired clerk.

"I'm here for the turtle snorkeling."

He had never been jealous of a woman before. But in that moment he was fiercely, horribly jealous of the clerk. Anika was smiling at her like she was a long-lost friend. She brushed a lock of hair behind her ear, giving him a view of the excitement sparkling on her face.

"We'll be heading out in about fifteen minutes. If you'll just sign the waiver and then head over, I have one other guest needing to watch the safety video."

Anika turned, her smile fading almost as soon as she saw him. Irritated, he shot her a cocky grin and raised his cup. She turned back to the clerk and pointedly ignored him as she signed the forms.

"Anika, I didn't know you were coming on this excursion," he said as she slowly walked over to him when she was done.

"Are you following me?" she asked as she stopped a few feet away, arms crossed. His eyes slid down to the curves of her breasts pushed up past the scooped neckline of her vivid red tank top. With her hair once again loose, a straw bag over one shoulder and blue jean shorts that showcased those long legs, she looked incredible. She followed his gaze, pink staining her cheeks when she realized what he was looking at.

"It's rude to stare."

He blinked, taking another sip of coffee to hide his satisfaction at the breathlessness in her voice. She felt it, too, this sudden attraction snapping between them.

"I apologize for staring."

She tilted her head, her eyes narrowed. "Why do I feel like there's a *but* in there?"

He grinned. "Because there is. But I won't apologize for liking what I see."

The pink deepened into a red that nearly matched the color of her shirt.

"Stop it. I'm not one of your conquests."

"I've never seen you as a prize to be won."

"Just my inn?"

Beneath the bravado, he heard the tiniest thread of something he hadn't picked up on before. Fear. Anika started to fidget as he watched her, glancing off to the side then down at her feet before her head snapped up and she squared her shoulders.

"What?"

"I'm just trying to figure you out."

"Well, don't. It's pretty simple. I don't like you. I'm not selling to you. End of story."

"Are you ready for the safety video?"

They both turned to see the clerk, who was standing just behind the desk with a wide grin on her face, her head swiveling back and forth as if she were taking in a tennis match instead of two people about to kill each other in her lobby.

"Yes," Anika said quickly. She stalked past Nicholas and sat down on a leather bench in front of the TV. Nicholas debated for a moment before he sat next to her.

"There's plenty of other seats."

"So pick one," Nicholas replied casually. "This has the best view and room for three or four people. I want to make sure I get all the safety information needed to enjoy this trip."

She grumbled something under her breath that sounded suspiciously like how she was planning to murder him on said excursion, but he ignored it. The clerk hit a button on the remote, shot them another silly smile and walked back to the desk as images of turtles swimming through the ocean filled the screen.

"I think the clerk might be playing match-maker."

Anika snorted and he bit back a laugh. He didn't know a single woman he'd dated who would have made such a derisive, uninhibited sound in his presence.

"Perhaps one of us should tell her that has as much chance as a snowball in hell."

"Snowball in hell," he repeated. "Another of your American euphemisms?"

"And an accurate one. Tell me," she said as her smile sharpened, "how does Hawaii measure up to the Caribbean? That was where you went after our last meeting, right?"

"Keeping tabs on me?"

"Hard to not overhear the maids gossiping about the fight you had with your girlfriend at a beachside restaurant. You were even trending on Twitter."

He grimaced. "Ex-girlfriend."

Ex-girlfriend and one of his few mistakes. Sadly, it had been a catastrophic one. Susan, a textile heiress, had entertained ideas of changing her status from millionaire to billionaire through marriage. An idea she hadn't shared with him until she'd slipped "insider information" to a magazine that Nicholas Lassard, the renowned bachelor, would be proposing within the year. He could have easily told her he had no interest in proposing. Had she bothered to ask him, he could have told her all of it in a private conversation instead of a public display on the beach of his latest resort. He'd tried to escort Susan to his office, but she'd insisted on being out in the open.

He scowled. He should have known she would have arranged to have the entire debacle photographed by a paparazzo. She hadn't gotten a ring out of him, but she'd gotten some photos of her looking elegantly tragic, soft blond curls framing her face, tears on her cheeks and her hands clasped together in front of her ample bosom as her white dress fluttered around her.

He suppressed a shudder. The thought of being tied down to Susan until death did them part was enough to make a grown man weep. The woman thrived on drama, on being catered to and taken care of, a quality that had initially drawn him to her. He enjoyed playing the role of hero. He just hadn't planned on doing it all the time for such a self-obsessed woman.

"I'm sorry."

His head snapped around. Anika was still staring at the screen, but her expression had lost its edge.

"For?"

"The breakup. Whether it was amicable or not, breakups are hard."

"Thank you." He took another sip of coffee to hide his surprise at the genuineness in her tone. He never would have described Anika as compassionate. Yet here she was, offering her sworn enemy words of comfort. "This one was for the best."

"Didn't lose the love of your life?"

"I will never have a love of my life. Susan, unfortunately, did not understand that."

Anika's body tensed next to him. He glanced over in time to see something flit across her face, something that made him feel, uncomfortably, like he had just disappointed her.

"Well, isn't she lucky you corrected her in that assumption." Before he could reply, she stood. "Enjoy the trip."

She walked out of the room without a backward glance.

CHAPTER THREE

STUPID, STUPID, STUPID!

Anika resisted the urge to physically smack herself as she stretched out on the trampoline mesh stretched between the hulls of the catamaran. The boat skimmed across the ocean, the sparkling blue waters of the Pacific passing by a dozen feet below her.

She was in Hawaii on the kind of trip she had always imagined. But instead of staring in awe at the islands dotting the horizon or the sharp, jagged peaks of the Nā Pali coast drenched in vivid green with waterfalls tumbling down from jaw-dropping cliffs, she was thinking, once more, about Nicholas Lassard.

I'm just trying to figure you out...

The memory of those words sent a shiver through her despite the sunshine warming her skin. When he'd looked at her like that, those blue eyes lingering on her body, followed by curiosity as if he had genuinely wanted to know more about her, she'd panicked. She didn't want a man like Nicholas taking an interest in her.

Not because she couldn't resist him, she reminded herself hurriedly. But something had changed between them. Yesterday on the pier, perhaps? Just now in the office? Or had something been there all along and they were just now becoming aware of it?

Whatever it was, it was dangerous. Nicholas was the enemy. And, thankfully, as he had reminded her, he was the exact opposite of what she wanted from a man. They had zero similarities when it came to what they wanted out of relationships. That she had been disappointed by his pronouncement of avoiding love was more than enough warning that she needed to stay away from him the rest of this trip.

The trampoline dipped. She turned her head to see a handsome man sitting down near her. His jet-black hair was buzzed short on the sides and long on the top. A light blue T-shirt clung to a muscular frame. His navy swim trunks were loose, but didn't hide the muscles in his legs that spoke to someone who kept himself in shape. He shot her a smile and she smiled back, waiting for her body to react.

Aside from a small, enjoyable warmth in her belly, there was nothing. Nothing even close to the heat that had bloomed low in her body and then snaked through her as Nicholas had raked his eyes over her.

Determined to banish Nicholas from her thoughts once and for all, she pushed up on her elbows.

"Enjoying the tour?"

"Oh, yes." His smile widened, flashing white against brown skin. "My uncle owns the tour company. I practically grew up on this boat." He held out his hand. "Adam Kekoa."

"Anika Pierce."

He hung on for just a moment longer than was necessary, appreciation warming his eyes.

"Your first time in Hawaii?"

"Yes, and I'm loving it."

"Good," he said with a hint of pride. "It's a beautiful island. Are you here for business or pleasure?"

"Mostly business. I own an inn and I'm here for a tourism conference."

The boat started to slow.

"Ladies and gentlemen, we're nearing our first snorkeling stop," the captain announced over the speaker. "We'll be issuing gear as soon as we stop. We have an even number of guests on board today and ask that you snorkel in groups of at least two."

"At the risk of sounding forward, do you have a snorkeling buddy?" Adam asked.

"No, but I—"

"Adam?"

Her pleasant feeling evaporated as Nicholas walked to the edge of the trampoline. Unlike Adam's casual attire, Nicholas still had on tan linen pants and a loose, grayish-blue collared shirt. He'd left the buttons at the top undone and rolled up the sleeves to his elbows, giving everyone a view of his toned chest and muscled forearms.

He should have looked prissy and spoiled. Not confident and sexy.

Adam turned, a small wrinkle forming between his brows.

"Yes?"

The sharp smile Nicholas sent his way nearly made Anika shiver.

"Your uncle asked if you would help him pass out equipment. One of his workers is helping a sick guest."

Adam frowned. "Okay." He glanced between Nicholas and Anika before seeming to come to a decision. "It was nice to meet you, Anika."

Anika waited until Adam was out of sight before she stood, gliding toward Nicholas with slow, measured steps as she fought the anger churning inside her.

"What the hell was that?"

"What?" The bastard had the audacity to look

completely innocent as he stared down at her. "I was talking with the captain. One of the guests got sick. He said he needed his nephew to help him. I offered to help and he pointed out Adam to me."

"I don't believe you for a second. You deliberately interfered because you saw that I was enjoying myself."

He sighed, as if he had the right to be impatient with her. "I did not poison anyone, Anika. I did not lie to Adam."

When he said it like that, her suspicions did sound foolish. But there had been something in his expression, something predatory when he'd looked at Adam, as if he'd wanted to wring the man's neck.

"Fine."

A wave smacked into the boat and sent it rocking. She started and stepped back, one foot landing on the trampoline. Nicholas snaked an arm around her waist and pulled her flush against him.

Oh, God.

Nicholas's body was hard and so deliciously warm she couldn't stop her harsh intake of breath at how good he felt against her. The press of his hips against hers, the hardness of his chest beneath her palms. The faint yet rich scent of his cologne, woodsy mixed with the warm, peppery smell of cinnamon.

She tilted her head back to tell him to release her. And froze.

His lips were less than a breath away. All she had to do was push up on her toes and they would be kissing.

She really wanted to kiss him.

Torn between the desire that had taken root inside her and panic that skittered through her, she lifted her eyes up to his. He was staring down at her, that greedy gleam back and burning in the blue depths, his fingers pressing possessively into her bare back and scorching her skin.

Then it was gone. He kept one hand at her waist and eased back. She nearly reached for him before she curled her hands into fists at her sides.

"Thanks."

"You're welcome." And just like that the casual, carefree Nicholas was back. "Ready to snorkel?"

"Yes."

She started to brush past him, but he laid a hand on her shoulder.

"Looks like you're stuck with me."

"What?"

She whipped her head around and nearly

groaned. While she'd been fantasizing about Nicholas's abs, the rest of the guests had already grouped up. Some were already in the water, swimming about with their snorkel tubes bobbing above the surface. Another quick survey revealed Adam up top with the captain.

She sighed. Her stubborn streak demanded she go into the cabin or back on the trampoline and sunbathe, anything but go snorkeling with Nicholas.

But that would be the ultimate example of cutting off one's nose to spite their face. The conference registration had included several excursions. While she was looking forward to the waterfall hike tomorrow and a tour of a coffee estate later in the week, she'd been most excited about the snorkeling trip. She loved to swim in the lake back home. Missing out on a chance to swim in the ocean, something she'd never done before, and see a turtle up close wasn't worth it.

Minutes later, she slipped off the ladder and into the water. Her body, used to the chilly waters of Lake Bled, acclimated quickly to the cool temperatures of the Pacific. She treaded water as she waited for Nicholas, purposefully looking away from how perfectly his black trunks clung to his backside.

Damn Irena and her sharp eyes for pointing out just how attractive Nicholas's rear was.

Once Nicholas was beside her, she struck out with strong, sure strokes away from the boat. She kept inside the perimeter of the bobbers the captain had tossed into the water but distanced herself from the other groups. A quick glance back confirmed that Nicholas was keeping pace with her. She made a downward motion and, at his nod, dove beneath the waves.

The quietness of the water surrounded her. Peace bloomed in her chest as the tension eased from her muscles. She hung, suspended, thirty feet above the sandy bottom, looking out toward the darker depths that went on for thousands of miles. A sobering and yet awe-inspiring feeling, she thought, to realize how much more there was to the world than her tiny corner of it.

Movement caught her eye. Wonder spread through her as she looked down and saw a turtle swimming beneath her. It was massive, the shell nearly four feet across, its flippers propelling it at a steady yet leisurely pace through the water.

Excited, she turned and grabbed Nicholas's hand, gesturing toward the turtle. His eyes widened as he glanced down. She saw his eyes crinkle as he grinned around his mouthpiece. Together, they swam down a little more, still keeping some distance so they didn't spook the majestic reptile, but drawing close enough to see detail like a strand of seaweed trailing in its wake, the small tail peeking out from under its shell.

She waited as long as she could until her lungs started to burn. With one last look, she swam up.

"Oh my God!" she cried as Nicholas surfaced next to her. "Did you see that?"

"I was right there," he replied wryly as he pushed his mask up onto his forehead.

"I know, but did you *see* that?" She laughed. "I can't believe it. That was just…oh, it was just incredible." She sighed in happiness and tilted her head back, soaking in the contrasting shades of the deep blue of the ocean and the paler periwinkle of the sky. "Best part of the trip."

"It's not over yet."

Something in his tone chased away her contentment. Something dark that hinted at unsatisfied desires and carnal pleasures. She kept her gaze averted as restlessness moved through her. Restlessness and a hunger that frightened her.

"Doesn't matter," she replied as she pulled her mask back down, as much a shield against the seawater as the man treading near her. "Definitely the best part."

When she turned to look at him, she felt her chest lurch. It wasn't just the desire in his eyes that had her contemplating swimming as far away from him as possible. No, it was how he looked at her as if he really saw her.

As if he knew what she was thinking, the wild thoughts running amok in her head, his lips curved up.

"We'll see."

"Immersing yourself in the communities you invite your guests to, experiencing what they will experience, can help you offer truly personalized, unique stays. Thank you."

Nicholas inclined his head to acknowledge the applause. His presentation on designing excursions and trips for his guests had been well received by the nearly four hundred attendees seated in the ballroom.

He'd also managed to keep himself focused the entire forty-five minutes. A feat, given that he'd spent the majority of yesterday and today thinking of Anika.

Something had shifted yesterday. Perhaps it was the visceral reaction he'd had when he'd been chatting with the captain of the snorkeling tour and looked down to see Anika in that damned orange bikini sitting next to another man. He'd never been the jealous type before, but had entertained a vivid fantasy of accidentally knocking the man into the water when Anika had smiled at him. When the captain had identified the young man as his nephew and mentioned needing his help, Nicholas had been only too happy to intercede.

He hadn't anticipated holding her, of having her nearly naked in his arms. But when she'd been there, he hadn't wanted to let her go.

Yet what continued to linger in his mind, late into the night when he'd gotten up to sip a glass of whiskey and gaze out his balcony doors at the moon casting silver shadows on the ocean waves, was when she'd spontaneously grabbed his hand, simply because she'd been thrilled by the sight of a sea turtle. And when she'd laughed, a look of pure joy on her face, he'd been hit with the realization that he had completely misjudged Anika.

Now, he was starting to genuinely like her. He needed to focus on getting the contract signed. But the more time he spent with her, the more he wanted to get to know her just a little bit more. Perhaps kiss her just once and find out for himself what she tasted like.

Probably for the best that as soon as they'd gotten back on the boat, she'd distanced herself from him and spent most of her time either in the cabin or on the trampoline at the front. Nicholas had given her space, needing a little for himself, too, to process how quickly their relationship was changing. Thankfully, Adam had been so busy helping his uncle he hadn't had time to approach her again. When the boat docked, Anika had hurried down the gangplank and driven off in her rental car before he'd even made it ashore.

He hadn't seen her since. A good thing, he reminded himself. It had provided him with a chance to take a step back from these feelings she stirred inside him and renew his focus.

"Thank you, Mr. Lassard." The moderator, a curvy young woman with a wide smile, gripped her microphone and turned to the audience. "We have ten minutes for questions."

Several hands shot up. Nicholas answered the questions with detail and a touch of humor. Public speaking, while not his favorite task, was a necessary component of serving in a leadership role. His father had made it clear that Hotel Lassard executives were considered the face of the company, a sentiment Nicholas agreed with. And, while he didn't care for it, he was good at it.

"Yes, the young lady in the back."

Awareness crackled over Nicholas's skin as Anika stood up, her slim form clad in a billowing yellow silk top and beige slacks that hugged her legs. With her hair pulled into an updo, he could see every line of her face, the long slender curve of her neck. Her mouth twisted into a small but devilish smile as she accepted a microphone from a conference worker. Anticipation flowed through him.

"You mention creating a one-of-a-kind experience for your guests by utilizing resources in the communities where your hotels exist, yes?"

"That's right."

"What happens when people in those communities don't like what your hotel is doing?"

He arched a brow in silent acknowledgment of the gauntlet she'd just thrown down.

"An excellent question. Understandably, not everyone is a fan of a world-renowned resort opening its doors." He added the slightest bit of emphasis to his words, savoring her narrowed eyes. "The biggest detractors are often other hotels concerned that we'll take away business."

"Don't you?"

Some people in the audience stirred, surprised by the unknown woman's audacity, but settled back down when Nicholas just smiled. God, she was glorious, standing there in sunshine yellow with lightning in her eyes.

"While it's inevitable that there will be some competition, the Hotel Lassard prides itself on community relations. That includes maintaining a team that travels ahead to any site prior to the beginning of construction and liaises with local hotel owners and managers. We strive to collaborate with them as much as possible."

"But what do you do when the interests of your hotel conflict with someone in the community? What then?"

If it had been just the two of them, he would have stood and applauded. She had him right where she wanted him, on the chopping block in front of hundreds of people. Her boldness excited him. Her daring impressed him.

And that beautifully haughty smile on her face made him want to pull the pins from her hair, tangle his fingers in the silky threads and kiss her senseless.

"It rarely happens. But in the event it does, we explore every possible avenue for collaboration. Not only is it not in our brand's interest to make enemies, but if we don't believe something is the right thing to do, we don't do it. You might argue," he continued as she parted her lips to do just that, "that we only do the right thing because the public is watching. And yes, especially in today's media-focused environment, the public is always watching. But we also do the right thing because it's the right thing."

"And what if the right thing is walking away?"

Challenge vibrated in her voice. The rest of the ballroom fell away as they stared at each other, two people at odds in every way except for the passion that had just flared from a simmer into a blazing inferno.

"The professional in me acknowledges that sometimes the right thing to do is walk away. But personally," he added with a wicked grin, "I don't lose."

The ballroom erupted into a frenzy of conversation. People craned their necks to see who had dared to take on the heir to the Hotel Lassard fortune, while others stared at Nicholas as they whispered and speculated.

Nicholas didn't pay attention to any of it. He just watched as Anika held his gaze, tilted her chin up in a clear gesture of contest. He let his eyes drop down, caress her body from afar, then looked back up. She was watching him, defiance still radiating off her in thick waves.

But he also saw the rise and fall of her breasts beneath her shirt, the faint color in her cheeks, her own perusal of his body as he stood up.

He wanted her. And, while it probably killed her, she wanted him, too.

Securing her signature on the sale contract paled in comparison to his new goal. By the end of the week, he would have Anika Pierce in his bed.

CHAPTER FOUR

TWINKLING LIGHTS CRISSCROSSED the air over the flagstone terrace of the resort. Tiki torches burned brightly. Waiters passed through the crowds of guests with silver trays, some carrying hearty fare like smoked pork with fried onions and guava jelly, marinated ahi tuna and honey walnut shrimp, and others with sweeter treats like slices of chocolate haupia pie, brown sugar–grilled pineapple and small bowls of passion fruit ice cream. Sensual jazz played from hidden speakers scattered among the lush blooms edging the patio. Beyond the green lawn, the waves of the ocean glowed in the light of the setting sun.

Anika sipped on her cocktail as she glanced around. She had been waiting all afternoon and well into the evening for Nicholas to seek her out. Ever since their verbal sparring in the ballroom, she'd been waiting to continue their battle, anticipating it.

Except he'd disappeared after the presentation. She hadn't seen him in the afternoon sessions she'd attended, not in the hallways in between workshops, nor in the tour she'd taken of the resort before dinner. The longer he stayed away, the more on edge she'd become, waiting for the proverbial ax to fall.

It had, she thought grumpily, cast a pall over her afternoon. Although the workshop on marketing on a limited budget had been helpful. The tour had been informative and fun. Still, too often her mind strayed to how Nicholas had looked as he'd said the words that had made her body go molten.

I don't lose.

The memory sent a shiver down her spine. She'd gone to his session as a sort of reconnaissance mission. The more he'd talked, the easier it had been to summon her old anger and dismiss whatever anomaly she'd felt for him on the snorkeling tour. When she'd stood to challenge him, she'd felt prepared, confident.

With every reply, she'd felt her resolve tremble. With every smile he'd directed at her, she'd felt her body weaken. By the end, when he'd uttered those fateful words, she knew she had to do something to reclaim her dignity. Talking to him, reminding him that just because they had a pleasant swim in the sea didn't mean she was just going to roll over and sign the contract, proving to herself that she could handle a conversation with him without thinking about his body pressed up against hers, had been the perfect solution.

One he'd thwarted by disappearing for the past nine hours.

She took a longer sip of her drink, the light and tangy flavors of lime, pineapple and vodka lingering on her tongue. Why was she continuing to let that man consume so much of her time and energy? Especially when she was in Hawaii, a tropical paradise where she was meeting with hoteliers from around the world?

A drumbeat filled the air. Anika turned with the rest of the crowd as a line of dancers clad in strapless red dresses with thick skirts filed onto the terrace. All of them wore crowns of leaves on top of their hair, with leis of the same leaves draped around their necks and matching strands circled around their ankles.

A woman with silver streaked through her dark hair broke from the dancers and stepped forward, a smile creasing her face.

"Welcome, guests from around the globe. My name is Kalea and tonight I am honored to bring the art of hula to you." The side conversations fell silent as Kalea's voice rang out, strong and proud. "Once a means of communicating stories about gods, goddesses, nature and things happening in the world around us, hula suffered over the past two hundred years. It was once deemed illegal to perform in public places, discouraged for decades by outsiders and considered a mere tourist attraction in my grandparents' time." Her gaze roamed over the audience. "The history of this dance was nearly lost. But thankfully, it has been revived in recent years. Tonight, we share our culture with you."

Kalea stepped back into the line. A moment later the dancers began to chant in unison, the song ringing through the night. Anika stared, mesmerized by the sharp, coordinated movements, the smiles on the dancers' faces, the passion in their voices.

"Incredible, isn't it?"

She started as warm breath teased her ear. Her fingers tightened around her glass. She could feel him at her back now, just a couple inches behind her as they watched the dancers spin as one in a tight circle.

"Have you seen a hula before?" she asked.

"My father took my mother and me to one years ago. I have never before seen, and likely never will again, witness such precision and perfection."

"Hmm."

"What?" His voice rumbled through her body all the way to her toes.

"For once we agree."

His chuckle caressed her skin. She swallowed hard and tried to focus on the dancers as their hands wove a story in the air, their bodies moving in perfect harmony. At the end they paused before lowering their arms to their sides. Thunderous applause broke out. The dancers bowed. As they walked off, a small orchestra set up on the adjoining patio began to play. A sensual, jazzy melody wound its way over the crowd.

Slowly, Anika turned to face Nicholas. Her breath caught in her chest. His all-black ensemble, from his coat and pants to the collared shirt with the undone top button giving a tantalizing glimpse of his chest, made her think of a demon.

Or the devil.

The man had certainly tempted her in more ways than one over the last couple of days.

He returned her frank perusal with one of his own.

"You look beautiful."

Pleasure bloomed in her chest. She glanced down at her dress, an off-the-shoulder sky blue gown with a bodice that clung to her like a second skin until it flared into a waterfall skirt that showed off her legs in the front and fell in gentle waves in the back down to her silver sandals. She'd discovered it in a secondhand clothing store back in Bled and bought it for herself.

But the heated gleam of appreciation in Nicholas's eyes certainly didn't hurt.

"Thank you." She cleared her throat. "I was worried."

A smile spread across his face.

"About me? I'm touched."

"Worried I might have sent you running back to your penthouse with your tail between your legs."

He leaned down. "I think you're more worried that I'm not scared off, Anika. It would be easier, wouldn't it, if I was, instead of thinking about you constantly?"

Speechless, she stared up at him.

"I need to mark this on my calendar. The first time Anika Pierce has never had a witty comeback."

Thrown by the heat in his words, scared by her body's response, she latched on to the first thing she could think of.

"Don't think you can seduce me into signing that proposal, Nicholas."

The teasing light disappeared in an instant, replaced by a harsh intensity that made her swallow hard.

"Dance with me."

Her mouth dropped open. "What?"

He grabbed her hand and pulled her toward the dance floor. She opened her mouth to tell him to go to hell, tensed her arm as she prepared to yank out of his grasp.

But she didn't. Because a wicked, decadent part of her wanted one dance, just one, with the man who made her feel sexy and beautiful and vibrant.

He's still a colossal ass. Doesn't mean you can't enjoy yourself.

Comforting herself with that thought, she followed him out onto the terrace, placing her now-empty glass on a passing tray. People were dancing, most just swaying in place, although some executed a few complicated moves that made her eyes widen.

Nicholas suddenly turned to face her. She managed to stop before running into him, but his abrupt turnabout left her mere inches from his chest. He released her hand and she knew a moment of embarrassment. Had he dragged her out here just to make a fool of her? Was this payback for her grilling him at the end of his presentation?

And then he touched her. Electric shock spiraled outward from where he placed one hand, possessively, on her lower back. His other hand rested briefly on her hip, then drifted slowly up her side, his fingers nearly grazing but just barely avoiding her breast before they trailed down her arm. By the time he wrapped his hand around hers and spun her into a turn, anticipation beat a tempo so fiercely in her veins she almost felt faint.

"I don't use sex to get what I want."

His words penetrated the haze of pleasure that had descended over her. She blinked, then focused on the irate expression on his face.

"I find that hard to believe," she managed to retort.

He pulled her against his body as he spun her around a couple wobbling back and forth. His leg moved between hers, the intimate move making her breath catch, before he guided her away from the other dancers.

"When you and I have sex, Anika, it won't be for any reason other than we want to."

A dull roaring drowned out the sounds around her. Each beat of her heart felt magnified, thundering inside her body as she stared at him.

"What?" she finally managed to gasp.

"You want me. I want you."

"I never said I wanted you," she sputtered.

Nicholas watched her, his fingers pressing more firmly against her back, his eyes glowing with that same predatory light she'd glimpsed on the catamaran.

"You also never said you didn't. So tell me

now, Anika. Tell me you haven't thought about me kissing you. Tell me," he continued, his husky voice washing over her and sending sinful shivers racing over her body, "you didn't think about how we'd be together when you were in my arms on the boat. That you didn't imagine me tracing my fingers, my lips, over every inch of your incredible body."

Say something!

But she couldn't. Not when her imagination was conjuring up carnal images of her and Nicholas entwined, arms wrapped around each other as he trailed his lips over her neck, her breasts, his hips pressing against hers without any barriers between them.

"Ah." His smile deepened. "So you have thought about it."

"I..."

"I want you, Anika."

"You want my inn."

"They're two separate things."

"Not to me," she whispered, trying to hold on to her sanity. Trying to ignore that intoxicating woodsy scent, the way he looked at her as if he couldn't bear another night without her in his bed.

No one had ever looked at her like that. Not Zachary, not the handful of men she'd gone on dates with her first two years at university.

There had been some pleasantness with Zachary and their physical encounters, but nothing close to this. Nothing like the fire burning inside her, this deep-seated need to feel Nicholas's body join with hers.

The song ended. The crowd erupted into applause. Nicholas held on to her for a moment longer before finally releasing her and joining them. Someone called out his name and he turned his head for just a moment.

A moment was all she needed to melt into the crowd. She hurried inside the resort, taking the stairs two at a time up to her room. She raced inside, closing the door behind her and locking both the doorknob and the dead bolt before she yanked the dress off and tossed it into the closet. When she'd first purchased it, it had been a symbol, a sign that she was doing something for herself.

But now, every time she looked at it, she wouldn't feel strong and confident. No, she would feel heat. Heat on her arm where his fingers had danced and grazed before he'd captured her hand in his. Heat between her thighs when she remembered how she'd wanted nothing more than to surrender to the lust that had descended on her and refused to release its grip.

With a muttered oath, she pulled a plain cotton nightgown out of her suitcase, then pulled one of the resort's robes out of the closet and thrust her arms into the voluminous sleeves. The thick, plush material enveloped her body, covered her skin.

But it didn't eradicate the desire that lingered in her blood. It didn't banish the memory of how Nicholas had held her, of how she'd wanted him to do more than just whisk her around the dance floor.

Her fingers fisted in the silky coverlet. What was happening to her? Marija and the inn had been the priorities in her life ever since she had arrived in Bled. She'd been able to indulge in her love of traveling the year after she'd completed her studies at the Bled School of Management, staying close to Slovenia but experiencing locations like Italy and Austria. She'd wanted to travel more, yes. But after a year when almost no one had traveled, followed by the rash of repairs and Marija needing more help, she'd put those dreams on hold.

She'd been disappointed, yes. But there had been comfort in returning to the familiar, an assuaging of the faint sense of guilt she'd experienced at not being around to help. There had also been satisfaction in her work, the camaraderie with the guests, walking around the lake that always made her feel like she was in a real-life fairy tale.

And family. She'd always had family. First her mother and father, who had shown her what a marriage founded on mutual love and respect could be like. Then her mother, a woman who had survived the unexpected loss of her husband in a car accident and continued to shower her daughter with love. Followed by Marija, a grandmother she'd only met twice in person before Danica's passing but who had welcomed Anika into her home as if she'd been born and raised in Slovenia.

Until now. Now, except for the inn, she was alone.

Is that it? she asked herself as she pushed off the bed and stalked to the balcony doors. *Am I responding to him because I'm lonely?* She closed her eyes. *Please let it be as simple as that.*

Slowly, she opened her eyes. Her room was on the corner of the resort and overlooked Hanalei Bay and the night-drenched waters of the Pacific Ocean beyond. Lightning flickered in the distance, followed by a soft rumble of thunder.

She had a sickening feeling that the answer to why she found herself so drawn to Nicholas Lassard was far from simple.

A sigh escaped her as a fork of lightning stabbed down toward the water, briefly illuminating the white-capped waves. Which should she fear more? That Nicholas wanted her in his bed?

Or that she wanted to be there, too?

Thunder rattled the windows of the ballroom. Voices quieted for a moment, then rose once more as the rumbling receded. The band struck up another tune, a rendition of a popular pop song that made the ever-increasingly inebriated guests dance faster as they laughed, joked and enjoyed themselves.

It was the kind of party Nicholas usually thrived in. So why, he wondered as raised his glass to his lips, wasn't he out there with them? While he didn't let loose to the extent that some people were, he liked having fun. Meeting new people, sharing a drink with a beautiful woman, perhaps inviting her back to his room.

Except the only woman he was even remotely interested was nowhere to be found.

The whiskey hit his tongue, the oaky flavor pleasantly sweetened with sugar and enhanced with bitters. If he focused on the taste, the scent of orange curling up from the peel artfully arranged in his glass, maybe he could push thoughts of a certain feisty brunette out of his mind.

Except the shimmer of amber liquid in his glass reminded him of eyes crackling with fire.

The citrus fragrance catapulted him back to how she'd felt in his arms, how hard he'd gotten just touching her hand.

A woman appeared in front of him, stunning with her black hair falling over her bare shoulders in thick curls and a fiery red evening gown. Her lips curved up as she eyed him with appreciation.

"Are you here alone?"

"I am."

She stepped closer and laid a confident hand on his arm. "Would you like to change that?"

He stared at her for a long moment, willing himself to feel something for the woman at his side.

But all he could think about was Anika.

"As beautiful as you are, I'll have to decline."

She eyed him for a moment before removing her hand with a slightly disappointed smile. "Whoever she is, she's a lucky woman."

He grunted as the woman in red walked off, hourglass hips swaying enticingly back and forth. Judging by the look of near terror on Anika's face when he'd told her just where he saw this battle between them headed, followed by her flight from the dance floor, she most likely considered herself the unluckiest woman on the island.

But, he reminded himself as he took another

sip, as much as she had wanted to, she hadn't denied their attraction.

He'd been able to deny it himself up until yesterday. Once he'd held her in his arms on the boat, experienced the novel emotion of jealousy seething inside him, felt the quiet joy of having her grab his hand and share that incredible moment beneath the ocean waves, he'd accepted that he wanted Anika.

Maybe she needed a little more time. Maybe they needed to settle this business with the inn first so they could just focus on each other as individuals instead of business rivals. How Anika thought she could possibly keep the inn running by herself as the repair costs mounted and the building deteriorated around her was beyond him. She struck him as an intelligent, driven woman.

So why did she insist on holding on to this? Surely she wasn't so emotionally attached to a house that she would risk it falling into ruin rather than let someone else have it?

An ugly thought invaded. Perhaps it wasn't just letting anyone else have it. Perhaps it was just him.

His fingers tightened around his glass. Never had he been bothered by someone in his world thinking negatively of him. Being liked paled in comparison to being respected.

Yet the possibility that he was the primary reason behind Anika refusing to sign grated on him. Yes, he was tough but fair. Yes, he had high expectations, but his employees and his guests reaped the benefits of the standards he set. Had Anika's inn been thriving, or even just quietly succeeding, he wouldn't have approached her in the first place.

But it wasn't. It was failing. It was failing and he could save it. She was just being stubborn because, for whatever reason, she'd had a grudge against him from the second she'd met him.

He tossed back the rest of his drink. Yes, they needed to settle the sale of the inn. He had been coming at it from the wrong angles, talking up how it could benefit the Hotel Lassard and how it could help her financially. After seeing more of Anika's emotional side the past couple of days, what he needed to focus on was how he could preserve the inn, the legacy that was so important to her.

And then, once she saw reason and he had her name on the contract, there would be no more obstacles between them and finally enjoying each other's company, both in and out of bed.

He glanced down at his watch. It was just before nine. Early enough to invite her to join him in the resort's cocktail lounge for a drink.

He started to pull out his phone when someone knocked into him. A moment later his shirt was covered in red wine. He looked up to see a wide-eyed older gentleman with a thick beard staring at his chest in horror.

"I say," he said in a thick Australian accent, "sorry about that." He glanced down at his feet and frowned. "I didn't think I was that munted." Nicholas bit back a sharp retort as the man awkwardly patted him on the arm. "I'll pay for the dry cleaning."

"No need."

"I can afford it, you know. I own four hotels in Sydney. Four!" the man insisted as he held up five fingers.

"I'm sure you can. Excuse me."

Nicholas walked to the elevators. Thankfully, he had the carriage to himself at it climbed toward the top floor. A minor setback, but once he changed, he would call Anika and—

A jarringly loud boom sounded overhead, one so deep it made the walls of the elevator shake. A moment later the lights blinked out and the elevator ground to a halt.

CHAPTER FIVE

ANIKA STOOD IN the open door of her balcony as the storm rolled over the mountain and swept across the bay. She swirled her wine in her glass, tilted it up to her lips and smiled as lightning lit up the enormous clouds rising above the island. Rain began to pelt the resort, big drops that rivaled the thunder's roar.

It rained in Bled fairly regularly. But nothing like this, this wild unleashing of nature's power.

Exactly what she needed to distract her from her earlier musings.

Thunder cracked overhead, an earth-shattering blast that rattled the glass door of her balcony. The resort plunged into darkness.

She sighed and leaned against her doorway. She had lived through plenty of blackouts, from summer storms in the Midwest and the occasional tornado threat to snowstorms leaving her, Marija and their guests cozied up for a day or two while the old generator had kept the bare necessities running. There had been a touch of excitement during those blackouts, a feeling like everything had slowed down and she was co-cooned from the rest of the world.

Her phone rang. Irritated at having her moment interrupted, she pulled her phone out of her pocket and frowned at the unknown number.

"Hello?"

"Are you all right?"

She nearly dropped the phone. "Nicholas?"

His low chuckle washed over her.

"Were you expecting someone else to call?"

"No, just...how did you get my number?"

"I can't tell you all my secrets now, can I?" he teased, his voice husky. "But truly, are you all right?"

"Of course. Why wouldn't I be?"

"I wanted to make sure you were okay after the power went out."

Confused and touched by his thoughtfulness, she found the resolve she'd built up over the last hour starting to crack.

"I am," she finally said. "And you?"

"Stuck in an elevator."

"What?"

"When you're in the hotel business," Nicholas replied casually, "it's a given that at some point you will get stuck in an elevator."

Anika shuddered. The resort only had four stories, but the thought of being stuck in a metal box hanging a few dozen feet above a concrete floor sounded like a scene from a horror movie waiting to happen.

"Have you contacted anyone?"

"Just you."

"Nicholas," she said, exasperated. "I can't help get you out of an elevator."

"I know. I called to make sure you're all right. I'll get out when the power comes back on."

A beeping in her ear made her look down. She swore softly.

"What's wrong?"

"My phone's almost dead." She sighed. "I forgot to charge it last night."

"Distracted, Pierce?"

"Terribly. There's this pompous ass who won't leave me alone, and he's keeping me up at night."

"Do I keep you up at night, Anika?"

Flustered, Anika glanced out the window as the storm continued. His words from the dance floor washed over her. But instead of disgusting her, the memory kindled something deep inside her. A longing for intimacy. A hunger for passion, to experience the kind of satisfaction Nicholas promised with a single glance.

"Anika?"

"Yes?"

The word came out on a squeak.

"Good night." She heard the smile in his voice, could picture it vividly in her mind. "Sweet dreams, hopefully of me."

"Dreams of strangling you, perhaps." She paused. "What will you do?"

"Not much I can do. As much as I enjoy the Bruce Willis movie where he performs some impressive feats in an elevator shaft, I have no desire to be a stuntman or end up a smear on the floor. I know you would prefer otherwise—"

"Don't say that."

Silence fell. Anika wanted to take back her words, but she meant them. Much as Nicholas drove her crazy, and as much as she had loathed him before this trip, she'd seen a different side of him the past couple of days. Yes, he was egotistical and cocky and used to getting his own way. But he was also intelligent, confident and even kind. She'd seen him talking to a bartender, some of the employees on the tour boat, the "little people" so many looked past.

"I wish I had a pen."

"Why?" she asked quietly.

"To mark the day Anika Pierce no longer wished me dead."

"I don't think I ever truly wished you dead. Just…horribly maimed."

His laugh rolled over, pulled the breath from her lungs as she closed her eyes and imagined him lounging in one corner of the elevator, a seductive smile on his lips, a teasing glint in his ocean-blue gaze.

"Progress."

Her phone beeped in her ear again. She had maybe a minute left of battery if she was lucky.

"Where are you?"

"I told you. The elevator. I'm stuck—"

"I know," she replied impatiently, "but which one?"

"The last on the right on the east end of the building."

She mentally pulled up a map of the hotel.

"Stay where you are."

"Okay," he said slowly. "Not too hard to do when you're—"

Her phone died. Before she could lose her nerve, she ran her fingers through her hair and stepped into the hall. Emergency lights glowed white, illuminating her way down to the bank of elevator doors at the far end of the hallway. She walked up to the one on the far right and placed her hands on the cold metal.

"Nicholas?"

"Anika?"

She smiled, grateful to hear his voice reverberating through the door. "Thought you could use some company."

When he didn't respond immediately, her bravado started to slip.

"Thank you."

She let out a shuddering breath, surprised by how relieved she was.

"So…how are you?"

He huffed a laugh. "I've certainly been worse. What's it like out there?"

"Quiet. No guests out in the hall. I imagine if people aren't stuck down in the ballroom, they're in their rooms enjoying the ambience."

"Ambience?"

"The thunderstorm. It's perfect."

"Describe it to me."

Anika frowned. "What?"

"I've always pictured you as cold."

She frowned, more hurt than she liked by his comment. "I'm trying to figure out how, with compliments like that, you're considered one of the most eligible bachelors in Europe."

"I'm charming, I'm handsome and I'm ridiculously wealthy," he replied easily. "Cold and aloof was my first impression. But the more I get to know you, the more I realized how much more there is to you. You don't jump in headfirst like I do. You bide your time, evaluate, think, plan. So when I hear that dreamy note in your tone when you tell me a storm is perfect, it makes me very disappointed that I'm stuck in here and can't see your face. For something to bring that awe to your voice, it must be truly spectacular."

Shaken, Anika let her hands slide off the cool metal and stepped back. Her heart responded to the most beautiful words she'd ever heard by tripling its rhythm as she tried to rein in her runaway emotions.

"Am I wrong?"

"No," she finally replied. *Why,* she thought with some irritation, *are my eyes hot?* "I'm starting to see why so many women fall at your feet."

"Because of my handsome charm?"

She waited a moment, swallowed hard. "Because you know how to make a woman feel special."

"Feel?" His laugh reverberated through her as thunder boomed. "Anika, you are special."

Trembling, she sank down onto the carpet and tucked her feet under her. "Lightning's flashing over the water. It's this vivid scene of crashing waves illuminated for a moment in silver. The mountains make it look even more dramatic. And when I'm cozied up in my room, wrapped in a robe with a cup of hot tea or sipping a glass of wine, I feel like I could watch the storm for hours."

"Stunning." Nicholas paused. "My brother and I used to watch the storms at our home in Scotland. It was my favorite of the family homes, one my mother inherited and where we spent most of the first five years of my life before we moved to London. Stone, turrets all over, a massive fireplace in the library, perched on the edge of a moor with mountains in the background."

Anika closed her eyes, pictured two little boys with their faces pressed against the window as rain rolled across the grassy plains.

"What's your brother like?"

"He's dead."

Horrified, Anika's eyes flew open.

"Oh. Oh, Nicholas, I'm so sorry."

"It's all right. It was twenty years ago."

It might have been twenty years ago, but the raw grief threaded through his words told her he still felt it like it was yesterday.

"I'm glad you have memories with him," she finally said.

"Thank you. Since I've shared a bit from my past, why don't you share a bit of yours?"

"All right. What do you want to know?"

"How does an American girl from the prairie end up running an inn in Slovenia?"

She chuckled. "Put like that, it does sound odd." She traced a finger over the pattern in the carpet. "When I was twelve, my mother passed away from the same cancer that took Babica. Babica was the only family I had left. So I boarded a plane and flew to Slovenia."

"What about your father?"

"Killed in a car accident when I was five." She swallowed hard. "I don't have a lot of memories of him. But the ones I do have are good. My mother worked as a nurse in Kansas City. On days she worked, he would take me to school. We'd stop at a little bakery in town and get doughnuts." A smile crossed her face. "Doughnut Days with Dad. I'd forgotten he used to call them that."

"He sounds like a wonderful father."

Something in Nicholas's voice made her look up at the closed elevator doors. "What about yours?"

Nicholas took his time answering, finally breaking the silence with a sigh. "We're in a good place now. My father is still CEO of the company. My mother serves on the boards of several charities and volunteers at a library."

"A library?" Somehow she couldn't picture a woman swimming in the kind of money Nicholas's family had reading to groups of restless little kids.

"She loves reading, and she loves kids. It's been good to see how far she's come. They didn't take David's death well," he added, as if he'd sensed her unasked question. "Dad was gone all the time. Mom slept and popped pills. I spent most of my time in school or with the soccer team. It wasn't until I started university that they got better."

The image of two little boys at the window shifted to one grief-stricken child watching the storm alone. Her heart cracked. As someone who had always been surrounded by love, she couldn't fathom being a child left alone in the throes of grief.

"Nicholas…" She tried to come up with words of comfort, of support, of anything that didn't sound blasé or empty. "I can't think of anything else but I'm sorry. That sounds like hell."

His laugh was soft but harsh. "It was lonely. The cheeriest times were when we went on vacation. Brief escapes when we could be happy."

Realization hit her. "That's why you went into the family business, isn't it? Why you focus so much on experiences and such for your guests?"

Another period of silence passed, followed by a quiet chuckle. "I never thought about it too much. But yes. The best times of my life have been traveling. I want to give the best to our guests. Plus," he added in a tone more reminiscent of his usual arrogance, "I like to win. Always have."

She sighed. "You're awful, you know that?"

"You've mentioned something of the kind before. What have I done now besides make you feel wretchedly sorry for the poor little rich boy?"

"You're making me like you."

The words emerged, a truth spoken she couldn't, and didn't want, to snatch back. Before Nicholas could reply, something deep within the hotel groaned. The lights flickered back on. Startled, Anika got to her feet as the elevator doors parted.

Nicholas stood just on the other side, hands tucked casually into the pockets of his trousers, his shoulders thrown back in a confident pose that just a week ago would have grated on her nerves. But right now, with the intimacy of their conversation hanging in the air between them, his eyes glittering as he watched her with a possessive gaze, all she could feel was heat.

Smoldering, erotic heat. Making her chest so tight she could barely breathe.

"I have the top-floor penthouse." Nicholas held out his hand. "Join me. Let's watch the storm together."

She stared at his hand for a long moment. She should go back to her room. Yes, she wanted him. But he wasn't good for her. He wasn't what she wanted. And the more they talked, the more she got to know him, the more dangerous he was. She didn't want to like him. The more she liked him, the more she opened up to him, the harder it would be to walk away when the time came.

Which she would have to do at some point. Men like Nicholas Lassard didn't stay. Regardless of how high they took you, how much they charmed and seduced you, they always left with the remnants of a broken heart clinging to their heels.

The elevator doors started to close. Nicholas stepped into the doorframe. The doors shuddered, then slid back.

"One night, Anika. Stay with me for just one night."

He moved closer, his eyes fixated on hers. She watched as he drew closer, her body tight, blood pounding through her veins. If he had moved quickly, had shot her that trademark smirk or made a pithy, arrogant joke, she might have been able to reach deep down inside herself, grab on to some rational thought and pull herself together enough to walk away.

But instead, he reached up and cupped her face in one hand, his fingers settling lightly on her cheek in a gesture of tenderness that destroyed the last, tenuous grasp she had on reason. She leaned into his touch, a soft sigh escaping her lips as her eyes fluttered shut.

Warm breath whispered across her lips just before his mouth closed over hers. One last bit of sanity tried to prevail, to warn her not to surrender to the man she'd sworn to fight at every turn.

And then he circled an arm around her waist, pulled her flush against his body, and all rational thought vanished.

Her lips opened beneath his. His tongue slipped inside the wet heat of her mouth, teased her with long, slow strokes that elicited a moan from somewhere deep inside her. Her arms looped around his neck and she leaned into his embrace.

He froze.

Oh, God. How could she have thrown herself like that at him? Embarrassed by her overly enthusiastic response, she started to pull away. She would thank him for the kiss, coolly and politely, then calmly walk out the door so he couldn't see her shame—

He grabbed her hips and pulled her back against his body, then stepped back into the elevator and slammed his hand against the button to shut the doors. Her gasp echoed in the car as his hardness pressed against her most sensitive flesh.

He placed a finger under her chin and lifted her eyes up to meet his. "If you stay with me, I'm going to make love to you."

Go! He was giving her the perfect opportunity to turn and walk away. To lay down the boundary once and for all.

Slowly, he traced his fingers up one arm. Her skin pebbled beneath his touch. A shiver rippled over her as she started to breathe heavier, faster. His hand moved up, grazed the sensitive curve of her shoulder and neck.

Before she could reach out and grasp the flimsy threads of rational reasoning, he ran his thumb over her bottom lip. The hardened desire in his gaze became a softer glow, one that could only be described as wonder.

"You are so beautiful, Anika."

Her eyes grew hot again. When he'd said it earlier, it had made her feel sexy, sensual. But now, when she was standing barefoot in a robe thrown over a cotton nightgown, her hair hanging in uncombed waves over her shoulders, she truly felt beautiful.

She reached up and slid her arms around his neck once more.

"Make love to me."

CHAPTER SIX

NICHOLAS SWEPT HER into his arms as the doors opened to the penthouse. He kissed her again as he stalked into the suite, his lips possessive and dominating. She surrendered to his touch. Her pulse tripled as he carried her to the massive bed. Lightning lit up the room as he laid her down, white light illuminating his handsome profile. Giving in to impulse, she pulled him down and kissed the hard line of his jaw, nipped playfully at his neck. He shifted, moved his body on top of her and pressed her down into the silky embrace of the bed.

"If you keep that up," he growled in her ear, "this won't last long."

A husky laugh escaped her lips. Delighted that she could affect him, she arched her hips up, savored the hardening of his jaw.

"Do I tempt you that much?"

"Do you remember that day in your office?" he asked as he started to trail kisses down her neck.

"Yes," she gasped as he eased the straps of her nightgown down.

Cool air kissed her bare breasts. Suddenly shy, she moved her hands up to hide her nakedness. He grasped her wrists and pinned her arms above her head.

"When you tossed the pieces of the contract into the fire and looked at me with that smug smile, I wanted to kiss you." He placed his lips against the swell of her breast. "I wanted to push you up against the wall, wrap my arms around your incredible body and kiss you senseless."

"Why didn't you?" she asked, her voice hitching as he swirled his tongue over her skin.

"Because you would have smacked me."

"Or tossed you into the fireplace," she replied with a teasing grin.

He responded by sucking her nipple into his mouth. She cried out, arched into his embrace as her fingers slid into his hair and tightened in the silky strands. Pinned by the weight of his body, she could do no more than writhe beneath him as he licked, kissed and nibbled first one, then the other breast.

"Nicholas!"

He moved back up and kissed her mouth again. "I love hearing you say my name."

His fingers grabbed the hem of her nightgown. He tugged the material up, then tossed it onto the floor. The storm chose that moment to light up the room once more with a series of flashes, bright white revealing her in nothing but a pair of lacy black panties.

Nicholas pushed himself up and ran his eyes over her. She forced herself to lie there, to not reach for the sheet or a pillow. The almost savage expression of male satisfaction on his face eased her tension, rekindled some of her earlier feminine confidence. Slowly, she shifted her hips, smiled as fire flared in his gaze. Testing, taunting, she trailed one hand down her side, over her ribs, then teasing the hem of her panties.

Thunder rumbled, making the crystals of the chandelier above the bed shake. Rain started to fall again, a faint drumming that crescendoed into a roar. It was either that or the clamor of her heartbeat as Nicholas lowered himself back down and kissed his way from her lips down her neck, over her breasts, her belly and then lower still. He traced his tongue along the scalloped lace of her underwear. She trembled as anticipation pulsed in her, making her body feel as light as air.

He reached up, pulled her panties down over her thighs, her calves, kissing her legs as he did.

And then she was completely naked before him.

"You're still wearing clothes."

"Astute observation." He shot her a wicked grin as he settled his body between her thighs.

Her core throbbed as she watched him lower his head.

"It's not fair."

"Life's not fair," he replied as he pressed a kiss to her inner thigh.

"But…" Her words trailed off as he kissed higher, closer to her most sensitive skin. Nerves fluttered in her belly.

He glanced up at her. The sight of his dark head between her legs filled her with a perplexing tangle of apprehension and desire.

"What's wrong?"

"I…" She swallowed hard. "Just a little nervous. No one's ever kissed me…there. Before."

"No one?"

Another shiver wracked her body, one that left her weak at the possessive gleam in his eyes.

"No."

He watched her, waited, gave her time to tell him to stop. When she didn't, he lowered his head.

Pleasure speared through her, hot and so delicious it made her tremble. Her hands fisted in the sheets, moved restlessly as he kissed her, teased her until she was sure she was going to scream if he didn't do *something*.

And then he did, his tongue doing wicked

things as he licked and stroked and loved her with every touch. Her hands moved down, her fingers tangling in his hair once more as she pulled him against her. The lightness in her grew, pulsing hotter, brighter until she could barely stand the sensation but dear God, she couldn't ask him to stop, not now, not when she was so close.

He pressed his lips to her. She cried out his name as the lightness in her burst. Her hips bowed off the bed as her entire body hummed with pleasure. He gentled his caresses but didn't stop, not until she dropped onto the bed, her body limp and trembling.

Thunder rumbled again, softer this time but more potent, the sound rolling through her body. Dimly, she heard the rustle of clothing, the rip of a wrapper. She opened her eyes to see Nicholas standing by the bed, gloriously naked as he slid a condom onto his hard length. She stretched her arms above her head, a satisfied smile crossing her face as he watched her every move with obsessive precision.

"You're very handsome, Nicholas."

He smiled down at her. "Thanks."

"I mean it." She rolled onto her side and let her eyes drift over his broad shoulders, the defined muscles of his abdomen, the tapered waist and thick thighs. "It's a little unfair that you have an actual six-pack, but given our circumstances tonight, I'm choosing to be grateful instead of jealous."

He stared at her for a moment before throwing his head back to laugh.

"How did I not see you before?"

Confused by the comment, she tilted her head. Then her bemusement disappeared as he wrapped one hand around his erection and stroked. Aroused, pleasure still sparkling through her, she rose up on her knees and beckoned for him to come closer.

He stalked toward her. Her body shuddered, eager to feel his naked skin against hers.

Except he stopped a foot away from the bed, still running his fist up and down his long, thick length. When she reached for him, he stepped out of reach and chuckled at her soft growl of frustration.

"Next time."

She planted her fists on her hips, one brow curving up. "What makes you think there will be a next time?"

He moved with predatory speed, wrapping his arms around her and pulled her flush against him. Every hard muscle, every chiseled plane, pressed against her nude flesh. The delicious intimacy of it scorched her veins as he slipped a hand into her hair and tugged so that she looked up at him.

"Because once won't be enough, Anika." He pressed his hardness against her wet center, a triumphant smile crossing his face as she moaned. "Not for this."

What if one night's not enough?

The thought sobered her, took the edge off her desire. Surely she would be able to walk away. She liked Nicholas, certainly more than she had. But that didn't mean she trusted him, or liked him enough to want to sleep with him again.

Besides, as he'd made perfectly clear in his own words, he wasn't interested in forever.

He tumbled her back onto the bed. The feel of his hard thighs pressed against hers banished coherent thought. Restless, seeking, she ran her hands all over his body, indulging in the greedy need to touch him. He indulged her, dropping heated kisses on her jaw, her neck, her breasts.

Emboldened, she skated one hand over his firm behind, trailing her fingers over his rock-hard thigh, sliding between their bodies to...

"Minx."

He captured her wrist and brought her hand up. He kissed the center of her palm, a gentle gesture that made her sigh, followed by a yelp as he nipped the sensitive skin with his teeth.

"Next time," he promised, the words a whisper against her lips.

Alarm pulsed through her, quick and frantic. Then she shoved it aside. *Not now.*

He rested himself against her liquid heat, then started to press inside. She gasped as he stretched her.

"Am I hurting you?"

"No, just…" Her fingers tightened on his shoulders. "You're big."

He leaned down and kissed her, leisurely and sweet, easing her tension away with soft caresses until she relaxed once more. Slowly, he pushed deeper inside her until his hips rested against hers, his entire length buried inside her. She tightened her body around him and smiled when his breath caught.

"Careful, *bhrèagha*," he said tightly, his Scottish lilt more pronounced.

"Where's the fun in that?"

His lips twisted into a devilish grin. "Very true."

And then he began to move. Languid, deep thrusts that made her moan and gasp. Her hands moved on his body, gliding over his damp skin before settling on his hips and urging him deeper. Sensation built, blazing brightly where their bodies joined before it spiraled throughout her body, growing brighter with each movement.

He slid one hand into her hair, growled her name before covering her lips with his in a greedy kiss that sent her careening over the edge. He followed a moment later, his body tensing above her, his groan echoing in her ears.

He eased himself down on top of her, their breaths mingling.

"Am I crushing you?" he murmured against her neck.

She shook her head, too sated to even open her eyes. She couldn't say how long they lay like that, sweat-slicked bodies pressed together, his fingers drifting up and down her body. His touch was deceptively light. Each stroke etched something into her heart, kindled a need far deeper and more terrifying than the lust she had just indulged in.

"I'll be right back."

Cool air replaced Nicholas's heated body. But this time, instead of a balm to her overheated skin, it was a cold reminder of what she had just done.

More like who you did.

She rolled off the bed, wrapped a sheet around her chilled body and moved to the balcony doors. The chaos of the storm called to the hurricane spinning inside her chest.

If it had just been physical pleasure, that would have been easy. If it had just been about the incredible orgasms Nicholas had given her, she could have walked away without a backward glance.

Rain lashed the windows. She slid open the door, sucked in a breath as cold drops soaked through the sheet. Beyond the waving fronds of the palm trees, she could dimly make out the white-capped tips of the waves. Churning, frothing, stirred up by something unexpected.

It hadn't just been sex. Not after the glimpse she'd gotten of his tortured past and the man he'd become despite the loss. Not when he had cradled her with such unexpected tenderness one minute, then claimed her body the next with his dominating kisses, his commanding touch. Not when he'd held her gaze, his eyes burning with something that went deeper than mere desire.

You're imagining things.

She had to be.

She sensed him before his hands clasped her shoulders, drew her back against his body.

"What's wrong?"

His voice pierced the clamor of the storm. She tensed.

"Nothing."

"Liar."

The word whispered against her skin, an accusation without menace, but unfortunately accurate. She wanted to draw away, to hide. To take the coward's way out.

Except her mother and grandmother hadn't raised her to run.

"I never saw you and me ending up like this." She raised her chin up, staring into the heart of the storm. "It's unsettling."

He tugged the sheet down enough to bare her shoulders. "Because of the contract?"

Her breath hitched as he dropped a kiss on the skin he'd just revealed. "That's part of it, yes. But we're not together, like dating. I've never slept with someone I haven't been in a relationship with."

His hold tightened slightly. "Oh?"

"Don't." Irritated, she turned and faced him, ignoring the frisson of awareness when she realized he was still gloriously naked. "Don't you pull that macho routine where you go caveman on me because I've dared to have one lover while you've been strutting around like a damned rooster for years."

One brow curved upward. "A rooster?"

Her eyes dropped down to his half-erect hardness, then back up to his face. "An apt comparison. There was a rooster that used to strut around the yard back in Missouri. You remind me of him."

"Should I be flattered or insulted?"

"Both. A rooster mates between ten and thirty times a day."

Both brows shot up. "That sounds tiresome."

"I imagine you have a similar history."

His expression darkened. He tugged her closer, one hand sliding down her back and firmly molding her body to his. An illicit thrill snaked down her spine.

"I haven't been a monk, it's true. But even in my more…active days, I didn't go to bed with a different woman every night or even every week. If I had lunch with an acquaintance or business partner, the tabloids acted like she was a part of my harem. I haven't been with anyone in months."

"You and your ex didn't have a fling for old times' sake in the Caribbean?"

He leaned back, a satisfied smile tugging at his lips. "Why, Pierce, I do believe you're jealous."

"I am not," she lied. Because, she realized with horror, she *was* jealous.

"It's okay if you are." The smirk disappeared as he dropped his head. "I am. I almost tossed Adam off the side of that damned catamaran for daring to be close enough to touch you. The thought of anyone kissing you, touching you the way I just did, drives me mad."

Another tremble wracked her body, this one a deep, delicious quiver she felt all the way from her chest down to the swollen, slick skin between her thighs.

"Why?" she whispered.

"I don't know." He grazed his lips across hers, a light caress that taunted, exerted control. "I'll figure that part out later. But right now, I just want to do this."

He ripped the sheet from her body. Shocked, aroused, she stood just beyond the doors of the balcony, the rain hitting her bare back. His hands framed her face, slid into her hair as he kissed her, lips moving masterfully over hers. Gone was the gentle lover, the sweet seducer. In his place was a conqueror, a man who wanted to ensure she would never forget the feel of his body against hers as he tugged her down onto the floor, the taste of him on her lips as his tongue plundered her mouth.

This was what she needed. Hard sex, no kindness, nothing that could draw her heart into the equation.

Just once more. To get him out of my system.

He slid his hands up the backs of her arms, started to roll so that she would end up beneath him.

No.

This time she was in control.

She pushed back, knocking him off balance. She took advantage of his momentary surprise, planted her hands on his chest and pushed him down. Straddling his hips, she delighted in the flare of lust in his eyes as he grabbed her thighs. She reached between their bodies and grabbed his erection. The feel of his bare skin in her hand made her gasp. A mad desire shot through her, to feel him inside without any barrier between them.

"Condom," he ground out. "End table."

Thank God one of them had enough rational thought. She stood up and grabbed a condom packet off the table. After he slid it on, she wrapped her fingers around him and slid herself, slowly, down onto his hardness. He hissed, his fingers digging into her thighs as he tried to urge her to sink down further. She resisted, rising up until he was just barely inside her, before she lowered herself again, each stroke sending physical waves of pleasure through her body as feminine satisfaction wound through her at the frustrated need on his face. The cold rain at her back heightened each sensation, made her feel wild and uninhibited for the first time in far too long.

Finally, she sank down onto his full length,

their moans mingling as they found their rhythm. He reached up and cradled her breasts in his hands. The light strokes, teasing touches, made her move quicker, reaching for that incredible peak he'd already brought her to twice.

They soared over it together. She collapsed on top of him, allowing herself the intimacy of being held by her lover as the storm continued to rage on outside the doors.

Anika blinked against the sun streaming through the windows. She mumbled her discontent and started to roll over, then sat straight up when she came face-to-face with Nicholas's smiling face.

"What are…?" Her voice trailed off as the night, and early morning, came back to her in a rush. "Oh."

"Good morning to you, too."

He surprised her by sitting up and pressing a soft kiss to her lips.

"Um… I didn't mean to fall asleep here. Sorry—"

"Don't hide from me, Anika. Not after what we shared."

Irritation replaced her embarrassment. "Excuse me?"

"I always knew you were a force to be reckoned with." His eyes warmed as they traveled down her naked body. She resisted the urge to cover herself with the sheet. "But the woman I saw last night was truly incredible."

What was she supposed to say when he sat there clad in loose black pants and nothing else, morning stubble dark on his cheeks? Her hands itched to reach out and feel the roughness beneath her fingers.

"Thank you."

"You're welcome." His face sobered. "I ordered room service. We need to talk."

"Ah." She looked away, detesting the faint sense of dread that crawled through her. "The four words every woman likes to hear."

"Anika—" He swore as a ringing noise cut him off. "Give me a moment." He rolled off the bed, crossed to the glass doors and stepped out on the balcony, pulling his phone from his pocket and pressing it to his ear.

Alone, Anika released the breath she hadn't even realized she'd been holding. Spying her robe and nightgown draped over the back of a chair, she hopped off the bed and made quick work of getting dressed. Once the robe was firmly belted at the waist, she let out a sigh of relief. Clothed, she felt more in control, like drawing on armor as she prepared to do battle against her enemy.

Except at some point Nicholas had ceased

to be the enemy. She bit down on her lower lip and glanced over at the balcony. He stood at the railing, his head tilted up toward the sky, his shoulders thrown back in a stance of confidence. Never had the sight of a man's naked back made her want to swoon before.

But it wasn't just his impressive physique or how he'd made her feel last night. His appreciation for the hula performance, his sharing the horrifically tragic circumstances of his childhood, had humanized him. He was still a cocky bastard, she thought with a small smile as she watched him start to pace back and forth, one hand gesturing as he talked. He didn't want the things she did, which made anything beyond what they'd shared last night an impossibility.

Before this week, that thought had made her roll her eyes and thank the heavens she wasn't the kind of woman who interested a man like Nicholas.

But now…now it just made her sad.

She turned away from the balcony. The only thing she could think of that he would want to discuss with her was the inn. Had last night changed his mind? Had he finally accepted her answer, was perhaps even coming to respect her as a fellow business owner?

The scent of coffee penetrated her musings. She inhaled deeply as she walked over to the cozy white table and chairs set up in one corner of the room. An emerald coffeepot sat next to a matching cup and saucer, steam rising from the spout.

With a whispered murmur of thanks, she started to pour herself a cup.

And nearly spilled it all over the table as she spied the manila envelope next to the cup with the words "Zvonček Inn Purchase Proposal" written in black marker across the top.

She should be angry, she told herself as she set the coffeepot down with trembling hands. Angry, not hurt. Furious, not humiliated.

The anger was there, yes. It paled in comparison to the painful sorrow that left her hollow. It had been reasonable to assume that Nicholas would still want to talk about the inn. But had he really thought she would roll out of bed, march over and sign on the dotted line simply because she'd slept with him?

A sickening thought made her stomach roll. Had he had sex with her to make her more receptive to his proposal? Done exactly what she had accused him of on the dance floor last night? Using the desire between them to get what he wanted?

I don't use sex to get what I want.

He'd looked so fierce when he'd said it, had made her feel guilty for even suggesting it.

Except he'd also uttered another phrase that circled round and round in her mind.

I don't lose.

She had told him repeatedly she didn't want to sell. Her refusals hadn't stopped his relentless pursuit, and all because he was egotistical enough to want part of his new property to be on the shores of the lake, her inn be damned if it stood in the way.

Grateful for the anger creeping in, she grasped it, wrapped it around her battered heart. She had let her guard down, had let loneliness and lust guide her actions last night. Despite trying to hang on to some semblance of reality, she'd struggled to hold herself back, to keep her emotions in check.

Really, she told herself as she hurried toward the door, this was the best thing that could have happened. She'd needed this reminder that there could be no future between her and a man like Nicholas.

Resolved, she walked out of the penthouse and closed the door behind her.

CHAPTER SEVEN

Seven weeks later

ANIKA DRUMMED HER fingers on the arm of the plush tufted chair arranged in front of the marble fireplace. Never would she have pictured herself sitting in the lobby of the Hotel Lassard.

But then she never would have pictured herself having a civil conversation with Nicholas. Dancing with him. Sleeping with him.

Having his baby.

Her stomach twisted. She was seven weeks pregnant with the baby of a man she once had barely been able to stand. The man who had brought her to incredible, dizzying heights of pleasure.

The man who had seduced her even as he sought to try and buy the one piece of her family she had left.

That wasn't totally accurate, she grudgingly admitted as she stared into the hearth.

She hadn't been just a willing participant in her own seduction. No, she'd been an enthusiastic contributor.

She sighed. She hadn't seen or even talked to Nicholas since the morning she'd walked out. She'd expected him to show up at her room demanding to know what had happened. When the minutes had turned into an hour, she'd glanced at her phone, not sure if she was hoping that he would call or that he wouldn't.

Her phone had stayed silent. Each passing hour without any communication told her what she needed to know. Whether Nicholas had slept with her to persuade her to sign the contract or not, what they had experienced had been a one-time thing. He had no intention of chasing her down.

Which is a good thing, she'd reassured herself as she'd hurriedly packed and changed her flight to an earlier time.

Yes, the night had been enjoyable. But it was just that: one night. Not to be repeated. Judging by how hurt she'd been at seeing the contract on the table, she was already in too deep emotionally. Any further intimate contact with Nicholas would just cause more pain. Some distance was needed.

Except that every time her phone had dinged the week following her trip, her heart had fluttered. Every time that it hadn't been him, she'd had to fight back disappointment.

So, she'd thrown herself into work, implementing the ideas she'd come up with from what she'd learned at the conference. The biggest change, adding a nonrefundable reservation fee like one of the workshops at the conference had suggested, had made her nervous. Not only had it not deterred guests from booking her inn based off some of the new social media campaigns she'd implemented, but she'd been able to use the fees to spruce up some of the rooms. Little touches, like new linens and hiring a local handyman to paint. But if she could keep this up, small steps, she just might make it.

We, she silently corrected herself as she glanced down at her belly.

She'd become aware of something different the week before Christmas. At first, she'd chalked up her bone-deep exhaustion to working hard and fitful nights when dreams of her time with Nicholas invaded. Then, as her stomach had rebelled every time she'd tried to eat breakfast, she'd assumed she was getting sick.

It hadn't been until the day after Christmas, when her breasts had felt swollen and heavy, that things had suddenly clicked. A visit to the doctor had confirmed that she was indeed pregnant.

She closed her eyes and let out a sigh. She'd

always wanted to be a mother. She had just assumed that title would come with marriage to a man she loved, and one who loved her in return. Not a one-night fling with an international lothario.

She'd spent the week after trying to decide what to do. Part of her didn't want to tell Nicholas. He had made it crystal clear on their trip that he had no interest in settling down. If she told him about the baby, it would cement a connection between them that would never be broken. Worse, it meant she and her child would become a part of his life, even if he wasn't physically present: the chaos, the constant media attention not if but when the news came to light, the other women who would no doubt drift in and out over the years.

That last thought had made her so nauseous she'd barely stumbled to the bathroom in time.

But her mother and *babica* had raised her to be truthful and honorable. Withholding knowledge of this magnitude would have flown in the face of everything she'd been taught. And if her child ever looked her in the eye one day and asked if she had told their father about them, she needed to be able to say yes.

A quick search online had revealed that Nicholas was in Dubai. Mercifully, the few tabloid photos she'd found online had shown him alone or with colleagues. It had been a simple matter to check the online gossip websites. When one article had touted that the "devilishly handsome Nicholas Lassard, heir to the Hotel Lassard empire" was on his way back to Lake Bled to oversee the final phases of construction and readiness before his newest hotel's grand opening in a few weeks, she'd called over to the hotel and confirmed that Nicholas was indeed on his way. The hotel had done a soft opening the first week of January and was hosting select, invited guests as it completed construction on some of the remaining rooms. Construction Nicholas was overseeing as he also wined and dined his elite clients. When the receptionist had asked why she was calling, she'd simply replied that she and Nicholas had attended the conference in Kauai together and she had something to give him. The receptionist had called back to tell her Nicholas would see her at seven o'clock.

A tiny smile tugged at her lips. Even if part of her was terrified, there was a small, villainous part of her that was looking forward to seeing the shock on his face when she dropped the news.

Awareness tickled the back of her neck. Her eyes opened and her head snapped up. Nicholas leaned casually against the fireplace mantel, his tall, lean figure draped in black, one leg casually crossed over the other. The angles of his face, from the sharp cut of his cheekbones and broad forehead to the tapered point of his chin, contrasted with the smirk lurking about his full lips. His hands were in his pockets, his deep blue eyes focused on her face with an intensity no doubt designed to intimidate.

"Well, well," Nicholas drawled. "I never thought I'd see the day you would set foot in my hotel."

She took a deep breath. "I never thought I'd see it either."

"Welcome."

He still smiled pleasantly, still sported a pleasant tone. But he was reserved, distant.

"Thank you." She looked around, taking in once more the Swarovski crystal chandeliers, the floor-to-ceiling windows that overlooked the circle drive outside, the fountain that would spring to life in the spring. "It's lovely."

"It is." He sat down in the chair next to hers, his nearness crowding her. "Frankly, Anika, after the way you left in Kauai, I'm surprised to see you at all."

She wanted to look away from his eyes, but forced herself to maintain his gaze.

"I should have at least said goodbye. That was unprofessional of me."

His reserve cracked as anger rippled off him.

"Unprofessional? You didn't walk out of a business meeting. You completely disappeared without so much as a goodbye after we slept together."

"Keep your voice down," she hissed. A quick glance around the lobby confirmed that no one had been close enough to hear.

"Afraid what others might think of you if they knew you'd fallen prey to my charms?"

"I saw the contract, Nicholas." When he just stared at her, his brow slightly furrowed, she curled her fingers into fists. "The contract for the inn. Were you just waiting for me to put my clothes on before you handed me a pen to sign?"

His face tightened. "Is that what you thought?"

"Hard to miss when you conveniently left it on the same table as the coffee."

He sat back in his chair, his head swinging toward the fireplace. He stared at the flames for a long moment.

"Yes, I brought the contract with me to Kauai. I had planned on using some of our time in Hawaii to convince you to sell." His gaze swung back to her. "I had looked at it before I came down to the terrace that night. I laid it down on my way out the door. I hadn't planned on you coming back up with me. Nor did I plan on springing it on you that morning."

She stared at him, confused. Was he telling

the truth? Had she misread the entire situation and acted like an adolescent teenager heartsick over her first crush?

"However," he said as he leaned forward, resting his arms on his thighs, "since you brought it up, we have unfinished business to discuss."

Fury surged through her. *Bastard.*

"No, we don't. Not in regard to the inn."

"So, what's the plan, Anika? You're just going to run it by yourself? No matter what you think you learned at the conference, it can't save the inn."

"I've already seen an uptick in reservations," she fired back. "I've been making improvements, upping our social media presence. It's slow going, but I'm doing it. And I'll continue to do it by myself."

"For how long? That building is one brick away from collapsing into a heap."

"Ah yes, the building you want so badly you're willing to pay triple the current market value. That makes sense."

"If you would stop being so bloody stubborn, you'd accept the help I'm offering."

She threw back her head and laughed.

"Is that what you call it? Help meaning buying out the inn that's been in my family for over one hundred years so you can raze it and make a replica of the monstrosity you've constructed here?"

His eyes darkened. "Careful, Anika. I'm proud of what I've built here."

The fight drained out of her as quickly as it had arisen. This was not how she'd pictured the conversation going.

"I didn't come here to fight, Nicholas." She glanced around as a couple wandered through the lobby, the man dressed in a black suit, the woman wearing a violet gown that probably had some expensive label sewed on the inside that made the dress quadruple the cost of what she'd worn in Hawaii. Acutely aware of her thread-bare coat and thrift store trousers, she stood. "Is there somewhere private we could talk?"

He sighed, a thoroughly disapproving sound that increased her exhaustion.

"Fine. My office."

She started to stand, readying herself for the moment ahead, when her stomach rolled again. She froze. Fear dug into her stomach, clambered up her throat until she could barely breathe.

"I changed my mind. I'm sorry."

She turned away. She wasn't going to be sick. Not this time at least. But she wasn't ready. Not yet. She needed time, a little bit more time, some distance from the nasty confrontation they'd just had.

She'd barely made it three steps before she swayed. Exhaustion, the lack of food, her nervousness about talking to Nicholas, all of it came crashing down at once. Before she could move, Nicholas stepped forward and circled an arm around her waist. Panic skittered as his hand clamped down, his fingers brushing her belly.

"What are you doing?"

"You look like you were about ready to faint."

With a firm hand, he guided her down the hall.

"There's no need to support me. I can walk just fine—"

"You were going to topple over," he said frankly.

She glanced up at him, confused by his surly tone. What had happened in the nearly two months since they'd parted? Where was the man who teased and laughed and barreled through life with a carefree smile?

"I don't need you to manhandle me," she argued, some of her earlier bravado returning. Much easier to fight with him than to worry about how he might react to her unsettling news.

"Given your penchant for not taking care of yourself and preferring to work as hard as possible until you're on the verge of collapsing, I'm going to take responsibility and ensure that you get off your feet before we talk."

"I said I didn't want to talk tonight."

"You can say whatever you like. But you're not leaving here until you've had a chance to rest."

She ground her teeth together as he escorted her behind the desk past a wide-eyed clerk and toward his office. He strode in, kicked the door shut behind him and guided her to the couch. She looked around the room. Plush leather furniture, pale ivory walls that matched the winter landscape outside the large windows.

Nicholas circled around his desk, a gleaming mahogany behemoth, and sat down, the ice-kissed lake at his back.

Had she thought the worst part was telling him about the baby? She'd been wrong. It intimidated her, but it was the right thing to do. Once she told him, and he reiterated that he had no interest in being a father, it would be done.

But their argument in the lobby had stirred up the emotions Nicholas had brought to the surface in Kauai, from their shared moment on the catamaran tour of the Nā Pali coast to the conversation during the power outage that had led her up to his room.

No, the worst part of all of this, at least in this moment, was that she wanted to believe him, wanted to believe that he had wanted to spend time with her, to be with her just because of who she was, not what she owned. She didn't like feeling this vulnerable.

She swept her gaze around his office, noting the various awards and pictures of him with famous people. Movie stars, politicians, CEOs of international firms. They came from two completely different worlds. All of the reasons why she had resisted him in the first place came rushing back. He had told her before that he had no interest in true love, no enthusiasm for the things that she wanted out of her life: a family, stability.

"If you think any harder, smoke's going to come out of your ears."

She sighed. "Always one with a quick compliment."

His lips quirked. She shoved away the sudden, deep desire to see him smile, truly smile like he had those months ago.

"I was just thinking of how different we are, that's all."

"Ah. Still going with how I'm nothing more than a spoiled man-child playing at the hotel game while you actually work for a living?"

She flushed under his scrutiny as he flung her words from the Hanalei Bay pier back in her face.

"Contrary to this image you have of me of some rich playboy who just swims in money in his bathtub every night, I do care about my company and the people I work with," he said, an edge to his voice.

Ashamed, she looked down and stared at her feet.

"I said some horrible things before." She swallowed her pride as she forced out her apology. "I'm sorry."

"Why?"

"Why?"

He stood and circled the desk, trailing his fingers along the surface. She watched, unnerved and fascinated by her body's immediate response.

"Why do you say things like that? Why did you run away in Kauai?"

"I already told you," she said, her voice breathless.

He advanced toward her, each step hiking the tension in her body.

"So why are you here now? What is it you want?"

Tell him! Tell him now and just get it over with! her brain screamed.

He stopped, staring down at her with his hands tucked in his pockets much the way he had been when the elevator doors had slid open and she'd fallen into his arms.

"Well," he finally said, "are you going to spit it out? Or are we just going to—"

"I'm pregnant."

CHAPTER EIGHT

BLOOD ROARED IN Nicholas's ears. He couldn't have heard her right.

"Come again?"

"I'm pregnant," she repeated, "and it's yours. I haven't been with anybody since our…encounter."

His heart pounded so hard it was a wonder it didn't beat right out of his chest. Disbelief was paramount, but beneath it churned shock and a heavy dose of fear.

When he'd come back in from the balcony to find Anika gone, he'd thought that perhaps she had gone back to her room to change. But as the seconds ticking by turned to minutes, he'd been faced with the fact that she had left. Snuck out the door and deserted him without so much as a goodbye.

It had grated, yes. It had been the first time a woman had ever left him like that.

But there had been more to it than simple ego. The hurt that had pumped beneath his damaged pride had been the driving factor in not reaching out to her. He didn't want another relationship anytime soon, not after the disaster with Susan. And if he ever did contemplate dating seriously again, it would be with a woman he could keep at arm's length. Not someone like Anika who stirred him up inside. A woman who made him feel possessive, jealous, borderline obsessed.

As the days had turned into weeks and then nearly two months without a word from her, he'd focused on work. Or at least tried to. How many times had he picked up his phone, wanting to text, to call, to hear her voice? Each time he'd set the phone back down. That he wanted to talk to her, not just enjoy her company over dinner or her body in his bed, was enough to convince him that she had done them both a favor. Continuing any association with her would have been inviting inevitable drama into his life when they would have to part ways.

As she'd told him, Anika was the kind of woman who wanted things he couldn't give.

Things like a baby.

His eyes dropped down to her stomach, concealed under a loose gray shirt. He swallowed hard.

"How? We used protection."

A light blush stained her cheeks.

"We did. But do you remember in the middle of the night…"

Nicholas's brain fumbled, trying to remember. And then the image came back to him with roaring clarity. He had turned to her in the night. They'd made love to each other with questing hands, seeking lips. At one moment, just one, he had slipped inside her before he'd remembered that he had not put on a condom. He had quickly withdrawn, peppering kisses down her breasts, her belly, over her hips, before he'd pulled out a condom and sheathed himself.

"It was only a moment."

"A moment was more than enough." She stilled, a distant look coming into her eyes, one that hinted at a pain she was trying to conceal. "If you want, I'm happy to provide a test and we can get blood work done so that you know for sure it's yours."

Nicholas was surprised to find that he didn't doubt a single word that Anika was saying. As little as they had gotten along in the beginning, the time that they had spent together in Hawaii had helped him realize just what kind of person she was. Even though he'd been angry and disappointed at the way she'd walked out, she was not the kind of woman who would make up a pregnancy. Especially, he thought to himself, a pregnancy with someone she could barely stand.

"I appreciate the offer." He walked back around the desk, needing the familiarity of his desk, something that made him feel in control. "What steps do we take next?"

"I'll continue to go to my doctor's appointments. I can keep you updated, of course."

"Updated?"

She frowned. "You told me from the beginning you had no interest in being a father or having a long-term relationship. I'm not going to make any demands on you."

Annoyance stirred inside him. Did she truly think so little of him?

"I'm not just going to stand by and live the rest of my life while you take care of our child by yourself."

Alarm flooded across her face.

"What do you mean?"

"I mean that I'm going to be involved."

"Involved how? I'm more than capable of taking care of this child by myself."

"How? You can barely keep your business afloat."

Too far, he realized as her expression morphed into anger.

"As I said," she replied in a chilly voice, "since I've come back, I've already increased reservations for the spring by fifteen percent over last year. It's starting off small, but it's working. Just like I told you it would."

He half expected her to stick out her tongue

at the end, she was so fired up. And damned if that didn't stir his blood, just like she had when she'd stood up in the middle of a ballroom full of people and sparred with him. Reluctant admiration filled him. He wanted that property and everything that it could bring the Hotel Lassard. Still, it was impressive how hard she was fighting to keep the inn up and running, how much she was accomplishing with so little. It also made him realize just how capable Anika would be as a mother.

His eyes drifted down once more to her belly. He'd never contemplated the possibility of having children before, despite his mother's growing hints in recent years. He'd only been eleven when David had been killed. But that event alone had cemented his commitment to never having children. He hadn't been able to keep his seven-year-old brother safe. How could he possibly trust himself with the responsibility of an infant whose existence would literally rest in his hands for the first few years of its life? Even if he could overcome that fear, he wasn't sure that he would ever be able to overcome the pain. The pain that had lingered from years and years of his parents drifting farther apart and wallowing in their own depression as he had been left to fend for himself.

His parents were good people. They had overcome the odds and eventually found their way back to each other, and to him. But that decade between David's death and their reconciliation had been lonely and bitter. If his parents had succumbed to loss and left him for so long, what would he do if he were to face a similar loss? Could he guarantee that he wouldn't do the same thing his parents had done?

That it was even a possibility had been enough for him to abstain from considering a family of his own. A child deserved more than he could offer.

Yet as the reality of the situation hit, something shifted inside him. He might not be capable of providing a child with the kind of love and happiness that so many fathers could. But he had plenty of resources at his fingertips to ensure the child and Anika would never want for anything. He owed it to both of them to at least try to be involved as much as he could.

"Look, I know this was unexpected." Anika started to rise from the couch. "How about we sleep on it and talk tomorrow?"

Her face went pale. Nicholas was on his feet and by her side within seconds.

"Are you all right?"

"Yes." She attempted to wave him off, but he eased her back down on the couch. "The doctor said everything is fine. Just the usual first trimester symptoms."

"You're staying here tonight. You are not driving home when you look like death," he added as she opened her mouth to protest. "You need to rest, for both yours and the baby's sake."

She glared up at him.

"Is this how you're going to get your way for the next seven months? By using the baby?"

"Yes."

His blunt answer surprised a laugh from her. "I'm too tired to argue."

"Good. The top floor rooms are finished. I'll take you up there."

"All right."

If she was acquiescing this quickly to his order, she definitely wasn't feeling well.

"Do you have any guests at the inn tonight?"

"No, not for a couple of days."

"Excellent. You can stay here."

"Don't push, Nicholas," she said with warning in her voice. "I'll stay here tonight. I'm not staying for an extended period of time. My home is at the inn."

He knew when to push and when to relent. For now.

"Tomorrow we'll have breakfast together and we'll talk."

"Talk," she repeated in a voice that said she would rather jump into the freezing lake.

"I promise not to bite."

His words charged the air between them. Was she thinking of the moment he was remembering, when she had been on her hands and knees before him, his hands tight on her hips as he'd driven deeply into her. She'd tossed back her head, her glorious dark hair spilling across her back as she'd cried out. He'd followed a moment later. As they'd drifted down from the aftermath of their shared pleasure, he'd gently tugged her up, pulling her back against his chest, tilted her face to his and kissed her. He'd nipped her lip, a playful caress that had made her moan into his mouth as he'd covetously run his hands up and down her body.

"Yes, well…" Anika cleared her throat. "Tomorrow, then."

Nicholas opened the door and gestured for her to go out before him. His hand tightened on the knob as her sweet orange scent drifted up, teasing him as she walked by.

He would do the right thing by Anika and their child. Including not indulging in this mad desire for her and upping the emotional stakes between them.

He could resist. Would resist.

Even if it killed him.

CHAPTER NINE

Aɴɪᴋᴀ ꜱᴛᴀʀᴛᴇᴅ ᴀᴛ the knock on her door.

"Coming!" she called as she glanced at the mirror and winced. Her face was pale, her hair a mess. She usually didn't bother about things like makeup. A simple brush through her hair, a dab of mascara and some tinted lip balm were enough to keep her going. But the prospect of seeing Nicholas looking like she'd just crawled out of bed made her feel embarrassed. He was used to glitzy, glamorous women clad in diamonds and sequins. Normally she wouldn't care. But right now, she did.

Damn hormones, she thought to herself as she moved to the door.

She twisted the knob, opened it and then stared as Nicholas smiled at her, a heavy silver tray in his hands. The brooding darkness that had clung to him yesterday was gone, replaced by his customary charm.

"Good morning," he said as he moved into

the suite. "We missed breakfast the last time we saw each other."

She rolled her eyes even as her stomach rumbled at the scent of food drifting up from beneath the silver dome.

"I woke up to find a revised contract out on the table after we just had sex, Nicholas," she ground out. "Of course I left."

"Or," he countered as he lifted the silver dome off, "you could have stayed and we could have talked."

"I didn't want to talk. I felt embarrassed enough as it was."

Slowly, he set the tray down and then turned to her.

"I'm sorry for that. I never wanted to embarrass you, Anika."

Surprised by his apology, she looked down as her cheeks heated. "Um, thanks."

"I have a proposal for you."

Her head jerked back up and she eyed him suspiciously.

"Given how I handled your last one, and the numerous times you've brought it up since, perhaps you should cut your losses."

"Not losses," he countered with a confident smile. "Temporary setbacks. However, I think you'll actually like this one."

"Arrogant of you to assume."

"I propose that we put the subject of the inn on the back burner since we have a more pressing matter at hand."

Loath as she was to admit it, she did like this proposal. While she would prefer to get the business of the inn solved now, she also recognized that discussing how they were going to handle the baby was more important, especially since Nicholas did not seem to be wanting to take the easy way out and let her raise the child on her own.

He pulled out a chair for her and she sat, her eyes growing wide at the sight of fresh fruit, eggs and pastries. Her stomach rumbled. The first time she'd had an appetite in the morning in nearly two weeks.

"I wasn't sure what you would be hungry for, so I took the liberty of ordering a little bit of everything. I've heard the first few months of pregnancy can be quite challenging."

She took a bite of toast layered with butter and jam, moaning at the delicious berry flavors on her tongue. When she opened her eyes, it was to see Nicholas staring at her, his gaze riveted on her lips.

"Everything okay?" she asked nervously.

"You have a bit of jam…here."

He leaned over, his thumb swiping across her lip. The little bit of intimacy made her blush.

Nicholas cleared his throat. Embarrassment filled her. Had he noticed her reaction? Or had their one night in Kauai been enough to sate his attraction to her? Was she just making a fool of herself by mooning over him?

"Tell me everything you know so far about the baby."

Focus. He was being responsible. She needed to respond in kind.

"I'm seven weeks along. Due in early August. They picked up a very faint heartbeat at the beginning of this week. In a couple of weeks, I'll go in for an ultrasound and actually get to see it." Suddenly shy, she looked down at her plate. "You're welcome to be at that appointment."

"I would like to be there."

"All right." She took a deep breath. "Nicholas, I'm not saying you can't be involved. It's just not what I would have expected based on our conversations in Hawaii."

"Which is fair," he acknowledged. "I want to be involved at least on some level. I'm not content to simply be a bank."

The way he said "bank" made her tense.

"I'm not going to be coming after you for money."

"No, but I am going to make sure that you and the baby are well provided for. And that, Anika, is nonnegotiable."

She wanted to argue with him. But if she was being practical, she knew that she could not provide everything that was needed for herself and the baby off what she was making with the inn. If she accepted his help, she would be able to continue to focus her resources on repairs and getting back onto firmer financial footing.

"Fine," she agreed reluctantly. "Thank you. But nothing over the top. I'd never want our child to feel like I was using their father for money."

Nicholas surprised her by reaching over and grasping her hand. "I know you wouldn't. Whatever capacity I'm involved in when it comes to our child, I'll make sure that if that question ever comes up, they know, too."

Touched by the gesture, she gently squeezed his fingers then pulled her hand away.

"Well, is there really anything else? Once the baby's here, we can set up some sort of visitation schedule. Maybe based on your traveling—"

"What about us?"

"Us?" Anika repeated.

"Yes, us."

"There is no us. We had a one-night stand. Now we have a baby." Her chest twisted as for one brief, mad moment she let herself wonder what it could be like if they weren't two completely different people. "That's the end of it."

"But that's not the end of it. For us, and this child, it's just the beginning. We should focus on how our relationship is going to evolve moving forward."

"Did you not hear me?" Anika asked, frustration mounting. "There is no relationship."

How was she going to do this?, she suddenly wondered. She had planned on doing this by herself. Now Nicholas wanted not only to contribute financially and potentially be involved in the baby's life, but he wanted to be part of her life, too? How was she supposed to move on if he was always there, either directly in her life or haunting the fringes of it?

"There will have to be some type of relationship if we're going to maintain a positive environment for our child. I don't want to just get to know our baby. I want to get to know the mother of my child."

She tensed. She was not going to allow him any further into her life than she had to. Not when doing so would just deepen the pain of what could have been but would never be.

"Where do you see this going exactly? Because we're not a good fit. I don't see us dating, getting married, any of that. I don't want us to be together just for the sake of the baby."

"I don't want that, either," Nicholas replied. "As I told you before, I have no interest in marriage. That doesn't mean that I don't think that we should still have a healthy relationship."

"Okay," she said, "but you're always traveling—"

"I was already scheduled to be in Bled through early February for the last bit of construction and the grand opening. With it being the newest property, I'll also being making trips at least once a month, if not more, for the year after that."

Was that supposed to make her feel better? That he was steadily encroaching on her peaceful existence? She'd thought after the hotel opened he'd be gone, off to his next hotel and his next adventure.

"While I'm here," he continued, seemingly unaware of her inner emotional turmoil, "I'd like for us to spend time together. Get to know each other a little bit better."

She arched a brow. "Better than we already know each other?"

His smile turned devilish. "I wouldn't say no to a repeat performance of what we experienced in Kauai. But we don't know much about each other personally."

Embarrassed, she looked away. She was carrying the man's child and yet she didn't know much beyond the small bit he'd revealed and what she'd read in the tabloids.

"Okay," she finally said. "How do you propose we get to know each other better?"

"Let's start with something simple. Dinner, tomorrow night. There's a beautiful restaurant just a little way around the lake that I've been wanting to try. See if it will belong in our recommendations list for our guests."

"Lunch."

He frowned. "How is lunch different than dinner?"

Because dinner feels like a date. And I can't think about you like that.

"It works better for me."

She returned his stare with one of her own, willing herself not to back down. He was already throwing her carefully organized plan into chaos. She could force herself to accept his desire to be in their child's life, even be moderately grateful for it.

But she drew the line at anything that would pull her back to the emotional brink he'd brought her to in Kauai. That one fleeting night when she'd seen just why women fell for him. When she herself had teetered on the edge of something far deeper and more meaningful than a one-night stand.

Anika, you are special.

"Lunch this time," he said, his voice breaking into her thoughts.

She started and felt a blush creep up her cheeks. She had the disconcerting feeling that he could see exactly what she had been thinking about.

"Lunch," she repeated. "Good."

"This time."

Nicholas gazed out over the water. One of the things he appreciated about Bled was the constant views of the lake. No matter where he went, the lake seemed to be always in sight. The castle, the church perched on the island, the Alps standing guard in the distance, all of it came together to create a fairy-tale magic. In the past three years, he'd focused on cities like Tokyo, Singapore, London and New York. Modern, forward-thinking cities with populations that flocked to the luxury offered by the Hotel Lassard.

But always in the back of his mind he'd envisioned branching out into communities like Bled. Smaller towns and cities that offered so much more than the standard five-star restaurants, museums and clogged streets. There was still luxury and glamor to be found, but against the backdrop of culture, of unique destinations one wouldn't find in the midst of a megalopolis.

Places like Bled. It was unlike any of the locations he had ever visited or opened hotels in before. The natural beauty reminded him of the trips to Scotland, of simpler vacations they had taken before David's death. A day at the beach in Cornwall, hiking at Killarney National Park in Ireland, weekend getaways to their home in Scotland. As much as the more glamorous, luxurious vacations of his teenage years had been fun, part of the enjoyment had been the respite from grief. True happiness, like he'd found on those family journeys, had eluded him thus far.

He had come to understand the driving force behind the obsession to possess the hotel, a realization that had come on the heels of his conversation with Anika during the storm, followed by far too much time to brood over the past two months. To succeed here, in a town that reminded him of those times, in a place that mattered, had become the most important thing in his life.

And yet, he thought as his gaze slid from the bare trees guarding the island church to the woman seated across from him, in just a short amount of time, it was no longer at the forefront of his mind. Her dark hair was gathered in a loose bun at the base of her neck that emphasized her cheekbones and large, golden brown eyes. She wore a collared white shirt with a row of pearly buttons down the center and a gray skirt. Before Kauai, he would have appreciated her figure but still classified the outfit as matronly. Now, with his intimate knowledge of what lay beneath the material, he was struggling not to entertain fantasies of unbuttoning her shirt, punctuating each undone button with a kiss to the skin he revealed.

His fingers tightened a fraction on his coffee cup. He forced himself to relax his grip. Judging by Anika's reaction to his quip about spending another night together, she would not be gracing his bed again. The attraction was still there. He hadn't missed the flare of interest in her eyes, the blush in her cheeks.

But she wanted to keep him at arm's length. Preferably, he imagined, even further than that if possible. She hadn't been excited about the possibility of him being involved with the baby. Not excited, but she'd accepted it. Something he'd been grateful for. If she had pushed back, he would not have hesitated to use every tool at his disposal to fight for a place in the baby's life.

What that place looked like was still to be determined. But he had a responsibility, and he would see it through. He would be there for his child as much as he was capable.

Although just how much he was capable of being there was yet another question he would have to figure out in the next few months. Because the more he'd thought about it, the more he'd realized that his initial approach of money and a modest presence in his child's life was no better than what his parents had done, especially his father. Henry Lassard had thrown money at the problem of his family's grief. Luxury vacations, a private home in Bora-Bora, a Ferrari for Nicholas's sixteenth birthday. That had been easier than doing the hard work their situation had required.

As he'd walked himself through that unsettling realization, there had also been the ugly sensation, something that twisted in his chest, when Anika had emphatically said that she did not want to be married to him. Ridiculous, because marriage was certainly not in the cards for him. Yet ever since Anika had left him in Hawaii, he had been able to think of little else but her. She had popped up at the most inconvenient times. He'd imagined what she'd say to a particularly pompous executive during a contentious boardroom meeting with the Hotel Lassard's board of directors in London, pictured her by his side as he'd walked down the lantern-lined Charles Bridge in Prague. One moment he'd missed her, and the next he'd been angry, even furious that she had walked out on him.

Anger was better. Anger was easier than contemplating how, or why, she had crept into the deepest corners of his heart.

No matter what he felt for Anika, the thought of continuing his life as a bachelor, of traveling around the world while she stayed here in Bled and raised their child, filled him with something almost akin to loss. Thinking about the trips he had lined up after the grand opening and into spring made him feel like he was already failing.

That was partly why, in addition to working on the hotel, he had spent the last day examining all the ways that he could do something. He had already set up a trust fund and savings accounts, and altered his will. Their child, and Anika—whether she liked it or not—would be well cared for. Taking steps like those, concrete measures toward ensuring they would have a comfortable life, made him feel like he was at least accomplishing something.

"Have you been out to the island?"

He refocused on Anika, watched as she moved a cheese and potato dumpling around her plate and frowned. She'd eaten some at breakfast yesterday, but she'd barely touched her dumplings or her salad. Wasn't she supposed to be eating for two now?

"No, I haven't." He glanced out the window again at the tall, dark spire of the church stabbing up toward the sky, the red-orange roofs of the other buildings surrounding it. "I've been on a tour of the lake, though. I'll make it to the church one day."

"It's an amazing bit of history," Anika said with a genuine smile that made his chest tighten. "Marija and I used to go there all the time. On the southwest side is a stone staircase with ninety-nine steps. Legend has it that if a groom carries his bride up the steps into the church, they can ring the bell inside and have their wish granted."

He smiled. It was stories like that, bits and pieces of history and culture that, coupled with the luxury of his hotels, made the experiences his family's company offered some of the best in the world. The tourism manager he'd hired had already added excursions to the island for future guests, but he made a mental note to schedule a trip to the island before the grand opening.

"Marija mentioned you two spent a lot of time out and about the lake."

"I didn't realize you two spoke that much."

"Only occasionally," he said, noting the defensive set to her shoulders. "In town a couple times, at a tourism meeting. And once at the Winter Fairy Tale market."

She relaxed and he forced away his irritation. Had she thought he'd been going behind her back, speaking to her grandmother and trying to convince her to sell? Or did she just not want him around her family? Thoughts of Marija stirred a sudden, fearsome thought.

"The cancer your mother and Marija had… is it genetic?"

"It is, but I'm not a carrier."

The tension that had seized his body loosened a fraction.

"I'm double-checking with my doctor, but the initial appointment I had said that unless you were a carrier of that gene, it's unlikely that our baby would be at risk."

Nicholas nodded. "This is all new to me."

"It's new to me, too," Anika said with a gentle smile.

"Let's talk about something positive. You seem to have fond memories of where you lived back in the States."

"I do. We lived in a small town outside of Kansas City just north of the river. The town was along the banks. Not mountains like this, but rolling hills covered in trees. We lived next to a large farm, but we also had a few animals— a cow, a couple of goats, chickens."

"Hence your knowledge of roosters."

"Yes." Anika grinned, the smile transforming her face. "My mother was a nurse, so we only kept a few animals. But it had always been her

dream to have a farm. Well, hers and my father's."
She glanced down at her plate. "I'm grateful for
what I've had. But it seems like as the years go
by, my family gets taken away from me bit by bit.
I missed having a father, especially when I would
come across something of his that told me a little
bit about who he used to be. Who he could have
been if he had been able to stay with us."

In that moment, Nicholas made a vow. To
Anika, to their unborn child and to himself.
He might not be the kind of father Anika had
pictured when she'd envisioned a family of her
own. But he would do what he could to give her
as much of himself as possible.

Her eyes glimmered as she looked out over
the water. He wanted to reach over to comfort
her, to pull her into his arms. A move a boy-
friend or lover might do normally. Not an ap-
propriate gesture for a couple exploring nothing
more than a co-parenting relationship.

He'd moved through his relationships, the occasional fling, with ease, confident in his every
action. But right now, seated across from Anika,
he wasn't sure what to do.

"It's the first time in my life I've been alone.
After my father passed, I had my mother. After
my mother passed, I had Marija. They were always there for me."

"I only met her the few times, but she was an

incredible woman. She told me a little bit about your family's history here."

"Yes. It's been in our family since just after the first World War. My great-great grandfather bought it for almost nothing off of an American who modeled it after his house back in Virginia, but then missed his home too much to stay. The house was a great source of pride for Marija."

"But not your mother?"

"My mother always told me that she enjoyed growing up here, that it was a beautiful place to live as a child, but that she wanted more. She wanted to travel, see more of the world. That's how she met my father. She was a traveling nurse, but she eventually settled in Kansas City when she got pregnant with me. At that point she'd been traveling nearly a decade and decided that it was time to grow some roots."

Nicholas cocked his head to one side.

"Do you ever get the feeling of wanderlust that she did?"

Anika shifted in her seat, as if his questions were making her uncomfortable.

"Occasionally. But not really."

She was lying. To him, certainly, but perhaps to herself, too. One day he would push her. But not today.

She changed the subject to his recent trip to the Czech Republic. They talked about his hotels, about the places they had visited. Lunch came to a close on a succulent dessert topped off with powdered sugar and cherries.

"This was nice," Anika said quietly as they were walking toward her tiny car.

"You sound surprised."

"I am," she admitted. "I wasn't expecting to enjoy my time so much." She smiled up at him, a shy smile that hit him right in the gut. "But I'm really glad we did this. Thank you."

"You're welcome. It was nice getting to know a little bit more about you."

"Maybe next time I can learn a little bit more about you."

"What do you mean?"

"You got to hear quite a bit about my past. How I ended up here, my parents. We talked about your hotels and your travels, but I didn't really get to know much about you."

He shrugged.

"That's who I am."

She frowned. "Who you are today, yes. But what about your past? Your family?"

He went cold inside. He'd just wrapped his head around accepting that he was going to be a father. He'd shared more about his past and David's death than he had with any woman he'd ever been with.

Why can't that be enough? he thought irritably.

"Perhaps later."

Her face fell a moment before she drew herself up, her eyes flashing. "I see how this is going to go. You get to hear about all my past, all the darkest parts of my life, but when it comes time for you to share, you're allowed to keep things close to your chest."

"I did share back in Hawaii. And you didn't have to share anything with me just now. That was your choice."

"Doesn't not sharing defeat the purpose?" she challenged him. "I thought this was about getting to know each other because we're going to be raising a child together. You're the one who made the choice to be involved, to push for us to spend time together."

"Yes, but as you pointed out, we aren't in a romantic relationship. Getting to know each other as much as we need to in order to be successful parents is one thing. We both have the right to keep other secrets."

She reared back as if she'd been slapped.

"You're right," she said stiffly. "Thanks for lunch. We'll have to do this again sometime."

A fierce wind whipped through the parking lot as she climbed in her car and drove away, piercing his clothes with icy fingers that left him cold on the outside. He preferred that to the coldness inside his chest.

CHAPTER TEN

A SHARP PAIN radiated up Anika's arm. She swore, dropping the hammer as she brought her hand up and sucked on her thumb. She'd woken that morning to a sky made all the more blue against the backdrop of a ground covered in a pristine layer of white.

The hope that maybe today would go by without anything bad happening had lasted all of seven minutes. She'd walked out onto the front porch and spied one of the thin pillars leaning precariously. The base had rotted through. If it wasn't fixed soon, the roof over the porch was in danger of collapsing. She hadn't budgeted for a repair like this, so she'd pulled out her hammer and tools. Marija had taught her many things, from cooking buckwheat dumplings from scratch to wielding a screwdriver. Skills necessary for running every aspect of a family-owned inn.

She'd waited until the sun had risen a little

higher and at least given an illusion of warmth outside before she set to work. She'd managed to get the roof of the porch jacked up and the pillar lowered onto the floor. She'd been working on prying out the rotten base for the past ten minutes. Frustrated with her lack of progress, irritated that her morning was quickly going by, and exhausted from her fight with Nicholas the day before—*not to mention growing a baby*—she'd made a stupid mistake and brought the hammer down on her finger.

She loved the house itself, loved aspects of her job. But when it came to things like this, balancing all of the to-dos that needed to be completed in order to make the inn successful on top of the administrative duties that awaited her, she didn't care for it. And that made her feel guilty. Guilty because she loved the house, the memories, the one remaining link to her family.

Guilty because the thought of running this place by herself, of putting dreams like traveling on hold while she clawed her way out of this hole, made her feel frustrated and helpless. It was why she had been so testy with Nicholas the day before. She had struggled to answer his questions about her desire to travel because until she'd gone to Hawaii, she hadn't realized how restless she had become. Growing up here as a child after losing her mother, she had craved the stability that living with Marija had brought her. Moving across an ocean to live in a new country had brought its own sense of adventure. She'd been happy here. When she'd first started to help with the administrative duties, she had been so focused on getting the inn back to its original state that she hadn't even been aware of any dissatisfaction.

In the months after Marija's funeral, she had chalked up her increasing negativity to depression, the natural progression of emotions after such a loss. How could the inn be a burden? It had been a connection to her past, to the incredible people wo had come before her, who had survived in this building for over one hundred years. That legacy, that connection to the past, had made her feel a part of something when she had felt so alone. After everything Marija had done for her, she owed it to her to keep the inn going.

So why now did she look at this building and not feel the excitement, the comfort, the sense of belonging that she used to? Why, when she looked at it as she was growing the next generation inside her, did she feel only defeated and exhausted?

It wasn't just her growing discontent with the inn or Nicholas's questions that had put her in a foul mood. It was his complete lack of sharing anything about himself. The man wanted—no, demanded—that she share herself with him. Yet clearly, he was not going to reciprocate.

As the pain in her hand subsided, she rocked back on her heels and glanced in the direction of the Hotel Lassard. Even with the trees bare of leaves, the woods were thick enough she couldn't see the hotel.

She had been enjoying lunch, even when he'd been questioning her about her feelings on travel. She had enjoyed listening to him when he had shared what little he had. Seeing his eyes focused on her when she spoke, it was yet again easy to see why he was so popular with women when he could look at one and make her feel like she was the focus of his universe.

A dangerous place for her mind to go, given that he had told her multiple times that he had no interest in taking their relationship beyond co-parenting.

Not that she had any interest in anything but co-parenting. She simply had not anticipated that Nicholas would have any interest in parenting on any level. He seemed like the kind of man to offer her a large check, ask for perhaps the occasional photo, and otherwise continue on with his life. That he wanted to be involved had both astonished her and warmed her heart.

However, after yesterday's argument, seeing

the extent of how much he wanted to get to know her but how little he was willing to share of himself, she'd wondered if Nicholas might be experiencing a change of heart. If not now, soon, perhaps.

The sound of gravel crunching made her look up. A red sports car pulled up in the circle drive. Her heart leaped into her throat as Nicholas climbed out of the driver's seat and circled around the hood, looking like an ad for men's luxury outerwear in a black peacoat and a scarlet scarf looped around his neck.

"What the hell do you think you're doing?"

Irritation edged out the awareness that had been spreading across her skin.

"Having a tea party."

He stomped up the steps and reached for the hammer. She leaned away.

"If you take this hammer from me, the next thing I use it on will not be a piece of wood."

"It's thirty degrees outside, Anika."

"Thirty-five and sunny with no wind. Makes a difference," she tossed over her shoulder as she turned her back on him and resumed her work.

"It's winter."

"Really? Is that why there's snow on the ground?"

A noise that sounded suspiciously like a growl came from behind her.

"You should be inside resting. Or eating."

"Eating?" She turned and frowned.

"Yes. You need to keep up your strength."

"And I will. But Nicholas, there are some days when I can barely stomach a cup of broth. It's normal." She gentled her voice as she saw the tension in his shoulders, the trace of helpless uncertainty on his handsome face. "I'm not going to do anything to endanger the baby."

He sighed and ran a hand through his hair. "I don't like seeing you work like this."

"Well, tough. This is part of my life."

"Do you want it to be?"

She narrowed her eyes. "I thought you said talking about selling the inn was off the table until further notice."

"It is. I'm not asking about selling. I'm asking if you personally want this inn to be a part of your life. Because the impression I got yesterday was it doesn't make you as happy as it used to."

Stunned, she stared at him. How did this man see so much about her? How did he know her so well, sometimes almost better than she knew herself?

"I'm not comfortable answering right now."

His eyebrows drew together. "Because I wouldn't share yesterday?"

"One, I don't have a good answer. And two…" She swallowed past the hurt. "I'm not comfortable sharing with someone who's only going to take and not give. It doesn't matter if you're the father of my child or my lover or my friend. I'm not confiding in someone who sees our relationship as a one-way street."

He stared at her for so long she wondered if he was going to say something or just turn around and leave.

"I'm going to stay and help you."

She cocked her head. "That's funny. What I heard was 'Anika, may I stay and help you?'"

His lips twitched. "Yes. That."

She let out a breath. "This kind of project isn't my favorite on a good day, let alone in the winter and two months pregnant."

He pulled off his scarf, crouched down next to her and looped it around her neck. That intoxicating mix of cinnamon and wood wrapped around her, warming her in a way the wintry sunshine had failed to do.

"Let me take a turn."

Something in his voice caught her. He held out his hand. Slowly, she handed him the hammer, accepting his offer of help.

"Thank you."

He nodded, something poignant flashing in his eyes before he turned to the pillar. By the time she came back out with mugs of steaming tea, he already had the rotted wood removed and was attaching the new base.

"How did you do that so fast?"

"My first job for the hotel was on the maintenance crew at our flagship hotel in London."

"Maintenance crew?"

He shot her a sexy grin. "Hard to imagine?"

With his coat tossed over a rocking chair and hammer in hand, no, it wasn't hard to imagine at all.

"Did you like it?"

"Loved it." He started to lift the pillar up. "When I was younger I loved tools. Getting the experience, seeing what our employees do, was eye-opening. And I still get to keep a foot in that door. Touring the construction sites, talking to the crew, the engineers, the architects."

She remembered the rough scrape of his palm on hers on the Hanalei Bay pier. "And doing some work yourself?"

He grinned again. "Boys and their toys. Sometimes it pays to be the boss's son and ask to get in on hanging drywall."

The insight into the father of her baby sent a small jolt of happiness through her. Just like their intimate conversation back in Kauai, she was learning more about the man behind the glamour and tabloid stories. A man that she was liking more and more. A man she could easily see teaching their son or daughter how to wield a hammer, how to swim, how to dance.

Her throat tightened. They wouldn't have the kind of family she'd dreamed about. But they could still be a family. Most importantly, her child was going to have a good father.

She held the pillar steady while he reattached the banisters on either side and brought the roof down. She walked down to the yard and looked back at the porch.

"Thank you." She smiled at Nicholas. "What a difference."

He came down the porch stairs and walked to her, stopping in front of her and looking down into her eyes.

"Come on a ride with me."

Emotion fluttered in her chest. "To where?"

"Somewhere special." He held out his hand. "You trusted me once today. Trust me one more time?"

The emotions spread through her, a confusing tangle that tied her up in knots. Hope, want, nervousness. It was a simple ride, not a marriage proposal.

Slowly, she slipped her hand into his, nearly closed her eyes as a sense of rightness filled her when his fingers curled over hers.

"Let's go."

CHAPTER ELEVEN

THE ROAD SLOPED UP, a gray ribbon curving through snow-draped trees. The Audi handled the turns with a smoothness that normally made Nicholas feel confident, in control.

He felt neither of those things today. And it was because of the woman sitting next to him. So close and yet just out of reach.

He'd mucked things up after lunch yesterday. Confiding in her back in Kauai had felt natural. It hadn't hurt that there'd been a solid steel door between them, allowing him to say the words he hadn't confessed to anyone while still keeping some sense of distance between them.

That hadn't been the case yesterday when she'd looked up at him with those big gold eyes, so willing to trust, to support, to offer him everything he'd craved as a grieving child yet had gotten used to doing without.

The possibility of opening himself up once more, of letting the true depths of his pain and fear not only see the light of day but be shared with someone, made him uncomfortable at best, if not downright afraid. What if opening the door to his past sent him spiraling like his mother or running like his father? What if Anika rejected him, agreed with his new and deepest fear—that he wasn't capable of being a good father to their child?

He'd gone over that morning to apologize, to try to put some of what he was feeling into words, only to find the pregnant mother of his child sitting on the porch in the freezing cold with a hammer. Yes, he'd admired her tenacity. But it had also angered him. Why couldn't the woman just accept help? Why was she so hell-bent on taking care of everything herself? On not letting him lend a hand?

Except she had accepted his help. And not just help on any project, but on her beloved inn. It had floored him to realize how much more impactful it was to help someone like Anika. With Susan and her constant needs, he'd gone from feeling like a champion to a crutch. With Anika, it hadn't just been his own desire to be needed. No, it had been that she trusted him enough to help that had nearly knocked him back on his heels.

He slanted a glance at her out of the corner of his eyes. Sun streamed in through the window, casting golden light on the strands that had escaped the loose bun at the base of her neck. The rich emerald color of the sweater she'd pulled on made her skin glow.

How had he not seen her before? Had he let his pride over her initially indifferent reaction to him blind him to who she was? What she was capable of?

"The castle is coming up," Anika said, her soft voice breaking the silence between them.

Nicholas glanced out the window at the orange-red roofed turret rising above the tree line in the distance.

"I haven't been."

Anika smiled. "It's worth a look. It definitely belongs on your recommendations for your guests."

Surprised, he looked over at her. It was the first time she had brought up the Hotel Lassard of her own volition.

"Why would you recommend it?"

"It's over a thousand years old. Small, but it has a nice museum, plus a wine cellar where guests can bottle their own wine. The restaurant is amazing. But," she said as her smile widened, "it's the view for me. The view is unlike anything else in Bled."

Nicholas flipped on his blinker.

"What are you doing?"

"What does it look like?" he asked with a grin. "With a recommendation like that from a woman who's basically a local, how can I resist driving by without seeing this incredible view?"

He saw the twitch of her lips even as she looked away. "Don't you have some billionaire stuff to do back at your hotel?"

"Billionaire stuff, no. Reviewing the latest reports on projects in Greece and England, including the status of delayed construction supplies and a summary from one of my engineers, yes."

He didn't miss the line that formed between her brows as he pulled into a parking lot surrounded by trees.

"Surprised I can read?" he teased as he opened her door for her.

"No." She bit down on her lower lip, a simple, unconscious gesture that sent a bolt of heat straight to his groin. "You're very different than what I expected when I first met you."

"I noticed your chilly reception."

She winced. "Sorry. I made some assumptions about you based on the way you dressed, the way you looked, the way women responded to you."

A satisfied smirk stole across his face. "So you were jealous."

"More wary," she said with a small smile of her own. "Bled is my home. I was afraid you were going to change things up too much, not understand the culture here and just blaze in with crystal chandeliers and diamond-encrusted silverware."

"I've never used diamond-encrusted silverware."

She chuckled. "I know. And everyone in town has said nothing but great things about you acclimating to the community. It's just...you're unlike anyone who's ever come here, at least since I've been here. Then when you wanted to buy the inn..." She sighed. "I don't deal with change well."

"I disagree with that." He glanced down, noted the surprise on her face as they crossed a small drawbridge and passed under a stone arch. "Look at what you're doing now, how quickly you adapted to the idea of becoming a mother. Pivoting to be the sole owner of the inn. Moving halfway around the world and adapting to living in a new country. I'd say you deal with change very well."

He glanced down to see her rapidly blinking. "Anika?"

"Thank you," she finally said. "It feels good to hear that."

He paid for their tickets, silencing Anika's protests by pointing out he had invited her on the ride and counted the visit as research. She grumbled but finally agreed and led the way into the lower courtyard, flanked on either side by the walls of the castle. In front of him, the cobbled gray stones of the courtyard ran up to a short wall with views of Bled, the lake and the mountains beyond. He breathed in, savoring the architecture, the history pouring out from every stone.

"Wait," Anika said, grabbing his arm as he moved toward the wall. "Your first view should be from the upper courtyard. Nothing compares."

He allowed himself to be pulled along, enjoying the excitement building on her face. It reminded him of how she'd been when they'd snorkeled off the coast of Kauai. When he'd gotten his first glimpse of who Anika truly was at heart.

"Why do you think you don't deal with change well?" he asked as she tugged him past a well with a shingled roof toward another stone staircase that curved back into the depths of the castle.

"Maybe a more accurate description is I don't like change," she said. "I used to. I used to feel adventurous. I wanted to travel the world like my mother, but I also wanted that home to come back to in between. But being away from the inn and Marija…" Her voice trailed off as she frowned. "Sometimes I felt scared, like if I was gone too long something would happen. Other times I felt guilty, that wanting to travel and not be as invested in the inn as Babica was made me a bad granddaughter. So, I'd come back and work twice as hard to make up for my absences."

"Based on everything I've seen, you're more than invested."

"I like parts of it. But other parts... I feel like I have to," she said as they started up. "Like if I don't keep the inn alive, I'll have let down the woman who was my family for over half my life and everything she worked for. Like I'm letting the last bit of my family die."

Before he could stop himself, Nicholas wrapped an arm around her shoulders and drew her close. She didn't even hesitate as she leaned into him. Their steps harmonized as they neared the top. Even as he kept her tight against his side and indulged in the sudden, fierce sense of possession, dread pooled in the pit of his stomach. He'd thought Anika's obsession with the inn had been a matter of pride, of not liking him and not wanting him to have it.

Learning the full extent of her reasons for not wanting to sell took his carefully laid plan that she'd already disrupted and tore it into tiny pieces. It didn't negate the fact that without a major intervention, the inn wouldn't survive.

Anika's shoulders relaxed beneath his arm as they neared the top. Feeling her against him, sensing the trust she was placing in him, was enough for now. The hotel would open in just a couple weeks, with or without the inn. He needed to focus on that, and the baby, for now.

"Are you ready?"

He glanced down at Anika, who smiled up at him with the same unabashed joy he'd first glimpsed back in Hawaii. His chest tightened as he entertained the idea of leaning down and brushing a soft kiss across her lips. The need to taste her, to mark her as his for everyone around them to see, shocked him to his core.

"I am. Although if the view doesn't live up to the hype, you owe me a drink."

She arched a brow. "And if it does, what do I get?"

"A full-body prenatal massage at the Hotel Lassard spa."

A sigh escaped her lips. "That sounds heavenly."

So did the idea of being the one to offer to massage her from head to toe. He bit back the invitation. Moments later they emerged onto the stone floor of the upper courtyard of Bled Castle. To the right and left were stone walls covered in barren vines, topped off by reddish orange roofs.

And in front of him…in front of him was heaven.

They moved to the stone wall at the edge of the courtyard. He released her and placed his hands on the cold rock, leaning forward to inhale a deep, cleansing breath of winter air. Beyond the wall there was nothing but a plunge straight down to a tree-covered slope several hundred feet below. The lake glimmered beneath the early afternoon sun. The church stood proudly on the island, and beyond that he glimpsed both the inn on the southern shore and the roof of the Hotel Lassard next door. Mountains rose beyond, smaller than the steep peaks to the north, but no less beautiful in the gentle rise and fall of their majestic summits.

"The first time I saw this lake, I felt like I was at home."

He felt Anika tense beside him. He didn't look at her, couldn't. Not if he was going to get through this. He kept his gaze focused on the snow-draped hills, the wispy clouds clinging to the tops of the taller peaks.

"David died when he was seven. We were riding bikes and a driver ran a stop sign." His bare fingers dug into the stone, the roughness grounding him in the moment, keeping him present even as the past tried to pull him under. "The driver was at fault. But to this day I replay that moment over and over in my mind. What I could have done differently. I looked away for a second and David rode his bike out into the road."

When Anika didn't say anything, he plunged forward.

"I know, logically, it wasn't my fault. My parents reassured me of that fact over and over as we sat in the hospital, waiting for David to come out of surgery, then waiting for him to wake up."

The memories washed over him. The incessant beeping of machines, the sharp scent of antiseptic, the tightness of his mother's grasp on his shoulder.

"That first year, we beat the odds. We went to counseling. My dad took us on trips. My parents spent every waking moment they could together. But something changed just before the first anniversary. My mother started sleeping in more. A couple nights I found her in David's old bed. The more she slipped into depression, the more work trips my father took. We existed like that for nearly nine years. The only times we were truly together were on our trips."

He looked down as Anika laid a hand over his. A simple gesture, but one that steadied him enough to continue.

"I haven't shared that part of myself with anyone. I've gotten used to keeping people at a distance because it was how I survived those years. Even after my parents reconciled, I kept them at arm's length." He steeled himself, looked down at Anika. "I don't know how capable I'm going to be as a father."

Slowly, Anika wound her arms around his waist and pulled him against her. He forced himself to relax, resting his chin on top of her head.

"I don't know how capable I'm going to be as a mother," she finally said. "But, from what little I've seen, you've got a lot of potential." She leaned back and looked up at him. She breathed in, then out. "I was scared when you said you wanted to be involved in the baby's life. I'm not as scared now."

It was one of the simplest compliments he'd ever received. Yet it warmed him like nothing else had in his life.

"But still scared?"

"Aren't you?"

"Terrified," he admitted with a small smile.

"Me, too. But you're not as bad as I thought," she replied, her eyes glinting with a teasing light for a moment before her face sobered. "Thank you, Nicholas. For sharing with me."

"You're welcome."

As he gazed down at her, the air shifted, heated between them. His eyes dropped down to her lips. His hands tightened on her hips as he heard the sharp intake of her breath. Slowly, he lowered his head. He didn't just want to kiss her, he needed to feel her mouth beneath his, to possess her once more—

A high-pitched squeal broke through the haze of lust. His head jerked up. A young man was kneeling on the cold cobblestones, his fingers clutched around a black jewelry box opened up to a glittering ring that a woman with black curls was currently gushing over.

Anika stepped back and looked away, her cheeks flushed.

"I should get back to the inn."

Part of him wanted to pull her back into his arms, to finish what they had started. But it was better this way, he decided as they moved away from the wall, to step back from desire. They needed to move slow, not give in to sensual urges that would distract them.

And, he decided as he followed her out of the courtyard, while he had confided in Anika, he needed to ease into whatever this relationship was slowly. Letting down his guard too soon, rushing in, could result all too easily in heartbreak.

CHAPTER TWELVE

ANIKA CLUTCHED HER hands in her lap, her eyes laser-focused on the clock ticking in the doctor's waiting room. Their appointment had been for fifteen minutes ago. She normally handled changes in routine very well. But damn it, she wanted to see her baby.

The door to the lobby opened. Anika glanced up, then did a double take as Nicholas strode in.

"Nicholas?"

The smile he shot her sent her heart catapulting into her throat. He walked over and sat in the chair next to her.

"You haven't gone back yet, have you?"

"No."

"Good." He glanced at his watch. "First time I've been glad a doctor has been late."

"What are you doing here?"

He frowned. "Today's the ultrasound, right?"

"Yes, but…"

"You did invite me," he reminded with a

slight smile that didn't quite reach his eyes. "I'm surprised," she finally replied. "Any time we've talked about the baby, you've been…removed." And he had been. Ever since their sojourn to the castle, he'd dropped by twice, once to take her out for tea, the other simply to check on her. He'd even mentioned reading a couple of articles about what to expect in the second trimester. But compared to the relaxed, enjoyable camaraderie they'd enjoyed that day, he'd been distant.

"After what you told me about David, I understand needing some time," she hurried to add. "I just thought this might be too much for you."

He watched her for a long moment before reaching over and settling his hand on top of hers. The slide of his skin on hers made her breath catch.

"I want to be here."

The sincerity in his eyes soothed away her words of protest. She realized that a part of her didn't want him there because she didn't want to get attached. She had started to, that day at the castle. But then he'd disappeared so quickly she'd wondered if she had imagined the deep intimacy she'd felt with him.

She didn't want him to show up, be a part of this journey, only to pull away later when things became real. Things like waking up in the middle of the night to feed a screaming infant or changing what seemed like a never-ending number of diapers. Nicholas might dominate boardrooms and offices around the globe, but somehow, she couldn't picture him balancing a squalling baby in his arms while warming up a bottle at one in the morning.

Still, she wasn't going to make him pay the price for her insecurities. They had months to go before they would face any of those obstacles. At some point in the near future, they would discuss what that first year would look like, the extent of how Nicholas would be involved.

But for today, she was going to focus on finally getting to see the life growing inside her.

The nurse called them back and escorted them into a dim room with a reclined medical chair. An ultrasound technician walked them through the procedure as she laid a towel over Anika's waist and spread a thick jelly over her abdomen.

"So, is this your first?" she asked cheerfully as she picked up a wand with a circular piece on the end.

"Yes," Anika replied, her heart beating fast as she watched the screen.

"Congratulations!"

"Thank you."

"Are you alright?"

Anika turned to see a concerned expression on the technician's face.

"I am." Anika let out a small, self-deprecating laugh. "I've always wanted a family and I just want everything to go well."

"I understand. Your first appointment went well?"

"Very."

"Then I'd say today is going to be great, too," the technician said with a reassuring smile.

Anika heard a rustle, then felt a hand come to rest on her shoulder. She looked up to see Nicholas gazing down at her, his expression serious. He didn't say anything, but he didn't have to. His presence alone settled some of the nervous energy zipping through her.

"Ready?"

At Anika's nod, the technician lowered the wand. She rubbed it over Anika's belly a couple times, her eyes fixed on the screen. Anika watched, waiting, her breathing starting to escalate as her mind whirled—

"There it is!"

Wonder filled her at the sight of the tiny creature on the screen. Pure, breathtaking wonder as she gazed at her baby.

"That's…"

"That's your baby." The technician glanced

at something. "Heartbeat at one-sixty, right in the range for healthy."

"So, everything's okay?"

Anika glanced up to see Nicholas staring at the screen, an unreadable expression on his handsome face.

"Everything's great."

His shoulders seemed to relax a fraction. Finally, he tore his eyes away and looked down at her.

"I've never seen an ultrasound before," he said, his voice muted.

She looked back, wanting to soak up every last moment. Her eyes trailed over the rounded head, the swell of the stomach, the teeny arms and legs.

"It's beautiful," she whispered.

"Beautiful and healthy," the technician pronounced. "I'll get you cleaned up and then you'll go back with the doctor to talk through everything. I'll print you off copies of the photos to take home with you."

As the technician shut off the screen, Anika stole another glance at Nicholas. He was watching the printer as it churned out photos from the ultrasound.

"Nicholas?"

He looked back at her, his expression unreadable. Trepidation whispered through her. Had the sight of the baby changed his mind? Seeing it literally in black-and-white?

The rest of the appointment flew by, with the doctor pronouncing both her and the baby healthy, as well as reassuring her that her levels of fatigue and nausea were normal for the stage of pregnancy she was in. Nicholas asked a couple of questions, but mostly kept silent.

At first, his unusual quietness made her nervous. But as the doctor gave her a rundown of the upcoming weeks, her earlier excitement returned and she tuned out Nicholas's presence. If he wanted to share with her later, he could. But she was not going to focus on him. Not right now, when she had so much to be joyful for.

Nicholas walked with her to her car after the appointment. She barely glanced at him, her eyes focused on the pictures in her gloved hands.

"Anika?"

"Hmm?"

"I'm going to follow you home."

She blinked and looked up at him. "You mean 'Anika, may I follow you home?'"

His eyes narrowed even as his lips curved into a reluctant smirk. "Yes. That."

She sighed. "Yes, you may."

Ten minutes later, Anika drove down the

lane. She'd barely parked the car when Nicholas appeared at her door and opened it for her.

"Do you have any guests tonight?"

"No. January is our slowest month," she said as he followed her inside. "I need to come up with something for next year's skiing season. Although," she added with a yawn, "I'm not disappointed this year. Half the time I can barely keep my eyes open."

"Why don't you head up to bed? I can lock up on my way out."

"I will in a bit." She hung up her coat and pulled the photos out of her pocket. "I think I'm going to make myself a cup of tea, light a fire in the library and stare at these for a while."

She looked up to find Nicholas watching her intently.

"You're happy, then?"

"Very." She crossed over to him and held up the photos. "How could I not be? I got to see our baby today."

She traced a finger over the tiny head, that sense of wonder returning. It might not be how she'd imagined starting a family. But it was happening. She was going to be a mother.

"I'll make the fire for you."

"You don't have to do that."

"I don't. But I'd like to."

She huffed to cover her spurt of pleasure. "Well, thank you."

By the time she walked into the library, a fire blazed in the hearth. Nicholas had turned on a couple of the banker's lamps, the green glass lampshades glowing in the darkening room. Nicholas himself had stretched out on one of the leather sofas.

Suddenly and inexplicably nervous, Anika walked into the library.

"I'm sorry. I didn't realize you were staying, or I would have brought another cup of tea."

"May I see the pictures?"

"Oh. Of course." She pulled the pictures out of her pocket and handed them over. He took them with a light touch, as if he were afraid he might rip them just by handling them. She focused on her tea as he shuffled through them. He would pause on one, turn it this way and that, then continue on to the next, still wearing that unreadable expression he'd had in the doctor's office.

Finally, he laid them on the coffee table and leaned back into the couch, staring at the fire.

"Is everything okay?" Anika finally asked.

"Yes."

Nicholas turned to her. He reached out, took the teacup from her grasp and set it on the table before turning back and taking her hands in his.

He's going to end it.

Anika sucked in a deep breath, mentally steeling herself. It had been too much, too much seeing the actual evidence that their night in Hawaii had created a child.

"I knew you were pregnant, had accepted it from the moment you told me." He glanced at the photos again, then back at her. "But seeing it…actually seeing the baby…hearing you say 'our child' cemented it." His hands tightened on hers. "I told you before I'm not sure what kind of father I'm going to make. But I know I'm going to try to be the best one I can be. For you and for the baby."

Anika stared at him. She'd been so prepared for him to tell her he couldn't do this, to walk out, that for a moment she couldn't process what he was saying. But as his words sank in, a cautious happiness began to spread.

"You've already been wonderful, Nicholas. The dates, reading articles, all of it—"

"Nice gestures," he agreed. "Ones I will continue to do. But I want to do more. I want to be more."

She gave in to temptation and reached out, cupping his jaw in one hand. "You will be, Nicholas. You are nothing if not stubborn. I know that if this is something you want, you'll make it happen."

His breath shuddered out. "Thank you, Anika. For trusting me. I know that's not the easiest thing."

"Neither is altering the entire course of your life."

"No. But—" a smile spread across his face, stirring heat low in her belly "—after seeing what I saw today, I don't want to be anywhere else but here."

She wasn't sure how long they sat there staring at each other, the only sounds the occasional crackle of a log in the fireplace or a creaking from above as the house settled. Did she move first? Did he lean forward?

Does it matter?

The thought flitted through her mind before their lips joined in a searing kiss.

Nicholas circled his arms around Anika's waist and pulled her closer on the couch. Fire shot through him as she moaned and melted into his embrace, her hands coming up to rest on his shoulders as he kissed her.

It had been two months since they'd last kissed. Two months since he'd held her like this. So much had changed, including the desire he felt for her. Back in Hawaii, he had been consumed by his need to take Anika to his bed. Yet the numerous times they'd made love that night had only made his hunger grow. Never had he let down his guard with a lover before, trusted her enough to take control and surrendered himself to someone's touch like he had with Anika.

The desire he felt now, while still laced with that ravenous edge that threatened to drive him mad, was deeper, even more possessive. Not just a carnal need to have her body joined with his, but a want for the woman who continued to impress him. When he'd seen the joy on her face as she'd seen their baby for the first time, heard the breathless happiness in her voice, something had shifted inside him. Something that now drove him to cradle her in his arms and force down the desire that threatened to overwhelm him.

He gentled his kiss, sliding his fingers into the thick silk of her hair and tilting her head back. When she moaned, he teased her lips with his tongue until she laughed, opening her mouth to him. He teased, coaxed, savored each taste, all the while wondering how he could have lasted so long without kissing her these past weeks.

"Where's your room?" he asked as he moved his lips down to the pulse beating at the base of her throat.

"Third floor."

"Of course." His hands moved to her waist, his fingers slipping under the soft cashmere of her sweater and settling on her bare skin. Just the feel of her sent a hot bolt of need straight to his groin. "Do you trust me to carry you up three flights of stairs?"

"I do, but…" She pulled back, a shy smile curving her full lips up. "Can I tell you one of my fantasies?"

"Considering how hard just hearing the word 'fantasy' from your lips made me, yes."

"I've always wanted to make love in a library."

The woman constantly amazed him. How had he ever thought her stuck-up and cold?

"Then let's make your dream come true."

He gathered her in his arms and laid her down on the plush rug in front of the fire. He pulled her sweater off and unclasped her bra, baring her plump breasts to his hungry gaze. She stared up at him with a mix of shyness and desire that drove him wild. He stripped himself of his own shirt and circled his arms around her waist. She arched up into his touch and pressed her body against his as he bent his head. He captured one nipple in his mouth, sucking and kissing and licking her as she moaned, her fingers digging into his hair.

He continued his sensual onslaught on the other breast before moving lower and unbuttoning her jeans. He slid them off slowly, kissing her from the swells of her thighs down to her slender ankles. But when he moved back up her body, she sat up and put a hand on his chest as he reached for the waistline of her panties.

"I go first this time."

Aroused beyond belief, he stood. She moved to her knees and unbuttoned his pants, sliding them over his hips with torturously slow movements. A groan escaped his lips when she wrapped her hand around the base of his erection. He looked down just as she licked him all the way to the tip.

"That feels so damned good," he growled.

Her smug look of feminine satisfaction made him harden in her grasp.

"Good."

She took him in her mouth, nails scraping lightly along his thigh as she sucked on him. His hands tightened into fists. Part of him wanted to let his body take over, enjoy the incredible sensations to the finish.

Next time, he promised himself as he finally pulled back and sank down in front of her.

"I want to feel you, Anika. All of you."

Her eyes widened as his meaning hit her.

"I guess we don't need birth control anymore," she said with a soft laugh.

"I'm clean." He reached out and grasped her hand, threading his fingers through hers and bringing her up to kiss her knuckles. "I had my annual appointment at the end of the summer. I haven't been with anyone but you."

The slow smile that spread across her face hit him square in the chest.

"I'm clean, too." She sucked in a trembling breath. "I told you I've only been with one other man. I've never made love without a…" A becoming blush stole over her cheeks. "Without protection."

That sense of possession returned, burned bright in him as his hand tightened on hers. "Neither have I, Anika." He turned Anika's hand over and kissed the sensitive skin of her wrist, savoring the shudder that ran over her body. "I want to make love to you without anything between us."

Slowly, she nodded. "I want that, too."

He lowered her back onto the carpet. Firelight bathed her body in a golden glow. She gazed up at him with faith in her eyes. His heart shuddered. Never had a woman looked at him with such trust.

It unnerved him as his gaze drifted down to her belly. He could take care of her, and the baby. Financially, he could ensure they wanted for nothing. But was he capable of being the man they needed, the father they deserved?

Anika raised her arms up, reached for him.

The simple action banished his unvoiced apprehensions. He couldn't have resisted her for anything in the world.

Their lips met, melded together in a kiss blazing with heat and some unnamed emotion that added a sweetness he had never known he craved until now. He pressed his body against hers, groaned when her naked curves molded to him. He reached down, placed his erection against her wet core and slowly slid in.

The sensation of sliding into Anika's molten heat nearly undid him. The intimacy of it stole his breath, as did Anika's sharp, beautiful cry in his ear. He dragged out each second, easing himself in inch by inch until he was fully joined with her.

He paused, savored the sensation of being buried inside the woman who had ushered in so much change to his life, who surprised and astounded him on a regular basis with her strength, her confidence, her resilience.

The woman who carried his child within her.

He started to move, long, slow strokes. Anika clenched around him, her hands moving over him restlessly as she rose up to meet his thrusts. When she cried out, he eased back.

"Did I hurt you?"

"Don't stop!" she gasped, her hands coming

up to grasp his shoulders in a fierce grip. "Don't you dare stop, Nicholas."

The sound of his name on her lips, along with her urgent plea, sent him higher. Fire built at the base of his spine as he succumbed to the spell woven by the incredible woman in his arms, the intimate setting, the glow of the fire. All of it combined, spiraled upward as Anika arched her hips up and took him deeper. A moment later her body tightened. Her nails dug into his back.

"Nicholas!"

She came apart in his arms, her skin flushed, her cries like music. He followed a moment later, heat spiraling through his body as he spilled himself inside her, groaning her name before he lowered his head and claimed her with a kiss.

He quickly rolled to the side and gathered her sweat-slicked body in his arms. She snuggled into his embrace, her head cradled on his shoulder.

"That was incredible," she murmured.

"It was."

Slowly, his hand drifted down over her breast, her ribs, then rested on the slight swell of her belly. He heard her breath catch, felt her body tense against his.

Then, slowly, she brought a hand up and laid it over his.

Emotion swamped him. The joy he'd seen on

Anika's face in the doctor's office had given him a glimpse of a future he hadn't imagined for himself since that day long ago on the streets of Belgravia.

He tightened his arms around her and glanced down. Her eyes were closed, her lashes dark against the paleness of her skin. The steady rise and fall of her breasts told him she'd fallen asleep in his arms.

His gaze drifted down to where their joined hands rested on her belly. Fear drifted up, tried to steal away the moment. Seeing their baby had strengthened his resolve to be a good father. But what if he could never let go enough to experience the same kind of happiness Anika had experienced today? Would he be able to give their child the kind of uninhibited love they deserved?

Heaviness tugged at his eyes. He gently moved away, pulled a blanket from one of the nearby couches and lay back down, draping it over them as he tugged her back into his arms. He pushed his fears away and allowed himself to relax, drifting off to sleep in front of a roaring fire with Anika safe in his arms.

CHAPTER THIRTEEN

ANIKA CURLED HER legs underneath her and sank into the plush embrace of the window seat in her room. She'd indulged in new pillows, a knitted throw from one of the shops in town and a small shelf she'd hung to hold her favorite books. Between the coziness of her nook and the deep blue waters of the lake stretching out before her, she was in heaven.

Her hand drifted down to her belly, her fingers spreading out. She didn't want to wish away her whole pregnancy. But she also could barely wait to feel the first flutters, the little movements as her baby grew. It had been two weeks since the ultrasound, and she wouldn't get another until she was twenty weeks along. She huffed, then let out a soft, exasperated laugh.

"I can't wait to meet you," she whispered down to the hint of roundness just below her navel.

Her gaze strayed toward the trees that separated the inn from the Hotel Lassard. Tomorrow night the hotel would have its grand opening. People from all over Lake Bled were invited, not to mention the entire world. Getting to know Nicholas, to see how much he invested in his work, had made it easier to talk about, and eventually become interested, in the Hotel Lassard at Lake Bled.

Unfortunately, it had also raised uncomfortable questions for her. Part of the reason why she had resisted Nicholas's offers before was because she had thought he simply wanted something because he wanted it. But seeing the passion that he had for his company, the passion that he brought to his guests and the time and attention he put in, altered everything. What if selling the inn to him was actually the best solution? Given what she knew about him now, perhaps he would do the right thing and maintain the integrity of the inn while doing all the things that she alone was not capable of. Her grandmother had wanted nothing more than for the inn to succeed. Was selling and letting someone else take over the reins to see it reach its full potential the right thing to do? Especially if it meant giving her more time to pursue not only motherhood, but her own hopes and dreams?

She shook her head. That line of thinking still felt foolish to her, still felt too much like sever-

ing the last remaining connection that she had
to her family. The further along her pregnancy
progressed, the more she desperately wanted to
preserve at least something for her child. Something of her history and her roots, where she
came from.

Now was not the time to think of it anyway.
She should be focusing on more immediate
things like her growing relationship with Nicholas. Ever since the ultrasound and that night
they first made love, they'd spent time together
almost every day. From her cooking him meals
to taking walks around the town and surrounding area, they had started to develop what felt
like a real relationship. That she had spent several nights in his bed, and he in hers certainly,
hadn't hurt.

A smile crossed her face. She'd woken up
that morning to his arms wrapped around her,
their bodies pressed together in her bed. Never
would she have imagined Nicholas Lassard of
all people falling asleep in a cramped queen bed
inside a centuries-old inn. But when she had
rolled over and found him looking deeply into
her eyes, felt his hand caress first her face then
drift slowly down over her bare breast, arousing
her to heights of passion she never could have
fathomed, it felt right.

Except, despite the growing intimacy between them, he still held back. Anytime she brought the baby up in conversation, whether by asking if he'd thought of a name or sounding him out on any ideas he might have about what he'd want to do the baby's first year, he would give a quick answer and then quickly turn the subject to something else.

She sighed. She needed to give him time. After all, he'd only been back in her life for about a month. Yes, she wanted more resolution, a clear idea of where they were going and just how involved he saw himself being. But they still had nearly six months to figure that out. Given all the progress they had made in such a short time, she needed to be patient and trust in the man that she was starting to learn more about.

Dimly, she heard a doorbell ring. Sighing, she tossed aside her blanket, thrust her feet into a pair of slippers and padded downstairs. She opened the door to a delivery worker, a silver box topped off with a red bow in her arms.

"Are you Anika Pierce?"

"Yes."

"Rush delivery. I need your signature that you received it."

"I'm not expecting anything," Anika said with a frown.

"It's from a salon in Paris," the delivery

worker said with a wide smile. "Maybe you have a sweetheart."

Heat suffused Anika's cheeks. She signed for the box and took it back upstairs, setting it carefully on her bed. She stared at it for a full minute, working up the courage to open it.

Finally, she huffed.

It's just a box. Open it.

The box was packed with red tissue paper, the same vivid hue as the bow. Sitting on top was a white envelope addressed to her in a strong masculine handwriting. What did it say about her, she mused as she picked the envelope up, that just the sight of his handwriting was enough to make her belly quiver?

She opened the envelope. A simple, plain card greeted her with the words "Thank you" emblazoned on the front. She opened it, her hands trembling.

The grand opening is tomorrow night at seven. It would honor me if you would join me as my guest.

She pulled back the tissue paper and gasped at the dress beneath. Slowly, she reached in and gently slid her fingers into the pile of frothy teal fabric. She moved to the mirror and held it up. With an off-the-shoulder neckline, diaphanous sleeves and a bodice that flowed out into a sweeping skirt, it was the kind of dress that would make a woman feel like a princess.

Not going and not supporting the man who had become so important to her in such a short amount of time was not an option. That he had taken the time and effort to do something like this, something he probably thought of as simple with the kind of money he had at his fingertips but that felt so generous with everything else he had going on, spoke volumes to her.

Yes, she told herself as she laid the dress out on the bed and stared at it with adoring eyes, there were still lots of questions to be answered. But for right now, the father of her child was thinking about her. He was including her in his life. And that was enough.

The hotel ballroom was packed. Guests in evening wear by Versace and Gucci milled about. Waiters slipped in and out of the crowds with silver trays loaded down with some of the finest delicacies European and Slovenian cuisine had to offer. Music from a string quartet drifted over the room, weaving a winter fantasy of airy music that enticed guests to linger and enjoy. It was exactly the kind of opening night Nicholas had envisioned.

Yet as he glanced around, he was disappointed. With how close he and Anika had grown over the past couple of weeks, he'd been confident she would have accepted both the invitation and the dress. They had still avoided the elephant in the room, the future of the inn. But he'd thought the relationship had progressed enough that she would at least attend.

"You look far too morose for someone who just launched one of the most successful hotels in Central Europe."

Nicholas turned and greeted his father with a smile and a hearty handshake. Henry Lassard surprised him by pulling him forward and wrapping him in a hug.

"I was just looking for someone," Nicholas said with a smile. "I can't be too upset when our reservations from April through the end of the summer are booked solid."

"I expected nothing less."

Nicholas returned his father's smile even as a thread of discomfort wound through him. He and his father had reconciled when Nicholas had approached him about pursuing a career in the family business. But there was always a faint distance anytime they spoke. It wasn't something he had paid much attention to, not until he had met Anika. Not until he had opened the door to his past. It was sobering to realize that he had never fully forgiven his parents for emotionally abandoning him in those years after David's death. It unsettled him, too, to realize that he had kept himself emotionally distant from his parents as well as from other people around him. A defense mechanism to not only protect himself from the pain of losing someone as he had lost David, but also as a safeguard against ever suffering the emotional tragedies he had when his parents had chosen their grief over him.

He grabbed a flute of champagne off a passing tray. If he was still holding on to this pain and resentment after twenty-plus years, was he capable of letting go and being the kind of man that he wanted to be for his child? It was a question he had been able to ignore as he had savored his time with Anika, everything from the intimacy of waking up next to her to simple things that he had never expected to get joy from, like looking across the table at breakfast and seeing her face smiling back at him.

But every relationship had its honeymoon period. And to date, every relationship that he'd been in had eventually lost that bloom of infatuation, of excitement and anticipation as it gave way to the cold realities of life.

"I hope Mother's fundraiser is going well," he said, trying to change the subject and focus on something other than his own morbid musings.

"The library had raised at least ten thousand

pounds when we last spoke." Henry glanced down at his watch. "That was over an hour ago. Knowing your mother, that amount has doubled, if not tripled by now."

The pride in his father's voice, the slight smile about his lips, stood out to Nicholas.

"Are you happy?"

His father blinked. "Happy?" he echoed. "But of course. Why wouldn't I be?"

"There was a time in all our lives when we were extremely unhappy," Nicholas pointed out. "I was just wondering if you and Mother are still in a good place."

Henry tilted his head to the side. "What's brought all this on?"

Nicholas shrugged. "Just curious."

His father looked down at the floor. "I would say, overall, yes, we're happy."

Coldness slipped over Nicholas's skin as he watched a small frown mar his father's brow. What was his father holding back? Had the past years been a lie, a front to hide that his parents had never truly moved on?

Before his father could answer, a glimpse of teal at the corner of his eye made Nicholas turn his head. His heart thudded hard against his ribs as Anika walked into the room.

The dress clung to the curves of her breasts, the sleeves whispering over her arms. The skirt fell in a fairy-tale froth of fabric to pool at her feet. She had kept her hair simple, lightly curled and pulled back from her face with silver pins to reveal her beauty. She glanced around, the nervousness clearing from her face when she saw him. The smile she gifted him brightened the room in a way no amount of crystal chandeliers or candles could do.

"Who is she?"

Nicholas turned to see his father's head swinging back and forth between him and Anika.

"Anika Pierce. She lives next door and runs the inn."

His father's eyebrows climbed up. "The owner of the inn you've been trying to buy?"

"Yes."

His father glanced at Anika once more. "Just don't lose sight of what's important."

Nicholas's chest tightened. Was he losing focus? He never would have thought that anything could derail him from his career goals, or his plans to propel the family brand higher then higher still. Yet someone had. Or rather, two someones.

The more involved he became, the more he would need to give of himself. He had committed to that, had thought that if his parents could achieve at least some healing, he could, too.

But now, as he watched his father be pulled away by a guest to discuss business, he couldn't help but wonder if he was reaching for something he was truly incapable of attaining. Every time the subject of the baby came up, he tried to summon enthusiasm, anticipation, something. Yet it was as if there was a wall built around his heart, an obstacle that no matter how hard he rammed himself against, he couldn't break through.

Would he ever be able to?

Anika approached him.

"You look beautiful."

"Thank you." She looked down, her fingers drifting over the skirt. "I've never owned something so beautiful. I can't thank you enough."

"You being here tonight and supporting the opening is thanks enough." He reached out, took her hand and pressed a kiss to her knuckles. "I know we haven't been talking business lately, but I appreciate you coming. I imagine it's not easy."

She cocked her head to the side. "A few weeks ago you would have been right. But the more I've gotten to know you and understand the reason behind why you do what you do, the more I've come to respect what you've accomplished here."

Never had someone's words meant so much to him.

"Thank you, Anika. Would you care to dance?" He smiled wolfishly. "Because I recall we never got to finish our last dance."

Anika rolled her eyes. "After everything we've been through, you still bring that up."

"I do have a reputation to live up to."

He led her to the dance floor. Two-story windows lined the wall and gave incredible views of the lake. With the faintest bit of color still splashing the night sky beyond the ridges of the Alps and the church on Bled Island standing proudly against the growing darkness, it truly was an enchanted setting. One brought to life by the woman in his arms.

This time as they danced, their bodies close together, the music winding around them, there was the sensual awareness of her body, of her breasts pressed against his chest, of her waist and how fragile it felt beneath his hands. But there was also knowledge there, knowledge of the woman and not just her body but her mind and her heart, resulting in the most intimate dance that he had ever shared with a woman.

Satisfaction spread through him. His latest hotel had opened to rave reviews. The event itself was a massive success. And he was dancing with a woman that he truly cared about. The woman who was carrying his child.

As they passed by a pillar, he saw his father speaking with an older couple. His pleasure dimmed. What had his father been about to say before they were interrupted by Anika's arrival? Were his parents still truly happy? Or was there something else going on beneath the surface, something that he had missed? The last two weeks, even as he had struggled to open himself up, he had reminded himself that his parents had walked through hell and come out on the other side. Scarred, yes, but alive and moving forward.

But what if they hadn't? What if they were simply putting on a show? If they couldn't overcome the grief of losing David, would he ever be capable of overcoming it himself? Capable of finally letting down his own barriers and allowing himself to be the kind of father their baby deserved? Of being the kind of man Anika deserved?

Anika's hand tightened on his arm. He looked down at her and returned her smile with one of his own. There were plenty of questions to be answered, yes. But not tonight. Tonight was about celebration, about joy, about looking to the future.

A future that, if he could just let himself feel, might include the woman in his arms.

CHAPTER FOURTEEN

EXHAUSTED, ANIKA LAID her head back against the chair in her office. Reservations had continued to climb, enough that she had been able to hire a handyman part-time. He was making improvements on the interior and had replaced some of the rotting boards on the front porch. If the weather forecast held and next week got as warm as they were expecting, the porch railing and trim might be restored to its ivory glory by the weekend.

Slowly but surely, she was reclaiming the inn bit by bit. Larger projects like replacing all the beds were still a ways away. But if she continued to make enough changes to bring customers back and kept up with marketing, the inn would survive.

It was an accomplishment, yes. But as her relationship with Nicholas grew, deepened, she was beginning to contemplate more and more the possibility of selling. Of starting a new chapter in her life.

Or, as she'd started to think of it recently, their life.

Don't jump in too fast.

Yes, the last few weeks had been wonderful. But it was just a beginning. There was still so much that had to be discussed and decided upon.

She'd stayed with Nicholas the night of the grand opening and woken up to an empty bed. Not surprising given all there was to do with the opening. She'd experienced a momentary flick of fear, along with a heavy dose of guilt. Had it been like this for him when he'd come back into his room in Kauai and found her gone?

But Nicholas had banished her fears by returning with a breakfast tray and sharing pancakes with her in bed before he'd planted a searing kiss on her lips as he'd headed out to a meeting.

The rest of the day had rushed by, ending on a somber note when Nicholas had received an urgent phone call about an emergency with his new property in Greece. He'd left quickly and she'd returned to the inn, not quite comfortable with staying in his suite without him there.

She walked out into the lobby. The thick burgundy-and-cream rug she'd found online stood out against the dark wood floors. Replacing some of the older lamps and having the handyman bring down some chairs she'd found in the attic had already altered the atmosphere from worn to cozy. Blankets made by a local artisan were stacked on one of the built-in shelves by the fireplace, inviting guests to relax by the hearth.

Regardless of whether she decided to sell or not, she was very proud of the work she'd managed to do in a short amount of time. If she sold to the Hotel Lassard, an idea she was entertaining more and more, she could bring the baby back for visits. She imagined picnics on the dock, walking through the fields of snowdrops in the spring and watching her son or daughter run chubby little fingers over the white petals, and was filled with a joy she had never experienced.

She glanced out the windows behind the desk that overlooked the lake. The island stood proudly in the middle, the church spire white against a pale gray sky. Snow clung to tree branches. The lake was still, smooth as mirror glass.

A peaceful tableau. One that reflected the growing peace she felt about the future. Things were certainly going in a different direction than she'd ever thought possible. But she was finding happiness in these unexpected turns, joy in moments she'd never envisioned. The more Nicholas did for her and the baby, the more she relaxed. When he did things like send her a basket with teas from a local shop she'd told him about in passing, it made her want a future with him in it. Not just a sideline participant who occasionally popped into her child's life to bestow the occasional gift before departing again for his bachelor life, but a man involved in the raising of his child.

A man who might want a life with her, too.

She moved to the fireplace, tossed in another log and sank down into a chair. Was she being foolish, picturing a future with Nicholas and their baby? They hadn't talked at all about the changes happening between them. But surely he wouldn't have said what he did at the opening if he didn't feel at least something for her.

I just need to talk to him.

As nervous as she was, a frank conversation would be in both their best interests.

A sudden rolling sensation in her belly had her on her feet and rushing for the bathroom. Dimly, she heard the bell ring over the front door, but she couldn't stop. She barely made it into the little room off the entryway before she was sick.

As she knelt on the floor, fire burning in her throat, she felt warm hands on her back.

"I'm here, Anika."

She closed her eyes against the hot sting of tears of relief that she wasn't alone.

"You're back early," she croaked as her stomach spasmed.

"Shush," he ordered. "Just focus on you and the baby right now."

For once she had no rebuttal, just listened as she heaved up the contents of her breakfast. Nicholas stayed with her through it all. When it was finally over, he escorted her back to the chair by the fire. She watched as he disappeared down the hallway toward the kitchen. When he emerged several minutes later, he had a glass of water in one hand and a cup of steaming tea in the other.

An odd sight, she thought fondly, to see the wealthy Nicholas Lassard dressed in a dove gray Tom Ford suit with a royal blue tie, serving her tea. He set the drinks on the end table next to her.

"One moment," he said with a smile.

Bemused, she watched him walk away again, only to come back with a small plate laden with crackers and slices of cheese.

"In case you need to replenish."

Touched, she swallowed hard. Then felt her

world shift as he leaned down and pressed a soft kiss to her forehead. When she looked up to see him smiling down at her, the truth hit her.

She was in love with Nicholas. From his trusting her with his darkest memories to how tenderly he'd cradled her belly after they'd made love, she'd been falling for him bit by bit for some time.

Shaken, she picked up the teacup and nearly spilled the hot liquid on her hand.

"Careful." Nicholas stepped forward and took the cup from her. "Are you still feeling sick?"

"Just a little unbalanced." She took a deep breath. "I think I'm okay now."

He handed her back the tea and sank down into the chair opposite her, glancing around as she sipped the lemony brew.

"The changes are nice."

Pleased he had noticed, and needing something else to think about other than her personal revelation, she smiled.

"Thank you. I got the new bedding in while you were gone. Took me a little longer to get the beds made, but they look wonderful."

He frowned. "You made the beds?"

"Yes."

"I thought you hired a new housekeeper."

"Part-time. I can manage until we get a little more money. Which should be soon," she said with a smile. "The spring reservations are up. Those nonrefundable fees have been a life-saver."

Nicholas nodded, his own smile slight. One hand came up, fingers curling into a fist that partially covered his mouth. As if he were physically holding himself back from saying something.

Surprised, she tilted her head. "What?"

"I'm glad you're happy, Anika."

"But?"

"I am concerned that continuing to manage the majority of the operations is taking its toll on you and the baby."

She suppressed the irritation that bubbled up inside her. She'd agreed to Nicholas being involved. She had ultimate say over her body, but she wanted to be able to have these conversations, especially when it involved their child, and consider Nicholas's thoughts and feelings.

"I appreciate the concern. I have cut back a lot. I've hired a handyman from Bled to take care of things like painting that aren't safe for me right now. I also have a front desk clerk and several more maids starting at the beginning of March, when business picks back up again." She took another sip of tea. "But right now, when it's just the occasional guest here and there, I see no reason to spend money on additional employees when I'm perfectly capable of laundering bedsheets and laying out a breakfast spread."

Nicholas's jaw hardened. "Noted. But how long are you going to go on like this?"

"Like what?"

He sat up and leaned forward, his body hard, his face intense. "How much longer are you going to play at innkeeper?"

Cold settled inside her chest.

"Play at?" she repeated, her tone frigid.

"We still need to discuss what happens after the baby is born."

"Yes, we do," she replied through tight lips. "And I have some ideas about that, some changes I've recently considered. For now, though, I have plenty of room here to raise the baby. And with the additional staff—"

"No."

Her spine snapped into a rigid line. "No?"

He gestured to the empty lobby. "You're by yourself a significant amount of time. How are you going to raise a child while caring for an inn that's on the verge of collapsing?"

Hurt spurted through her. "You just said the changes were good."

"Cosmetically, yes. But you can't keep going on like this, Anika. I think it's time you moved in with me."

Her jaw dropped. "Excuse me?"

"I have several more business trips in the coming months. I don't want to leave you alone here." He looked around again, his lips curled into a faint sneer as if he could barely stand to be in the room. Her heart twisted in her chest. "I'll book the penthouse at the Hotel Lassard for the foreseeable future. It's at your disposal."

"But I want to be here. In my home."

He pinched the bridge of his nose. "Your home is over a hundred years old and falling apart. Let me take care of this for you."

His words catapulted her back to autumn, when he'd stridden into her office like he already owned the place and pushed her to sell him the one piece of her family she had left.

"This isn't one of your business deals, Nick." She took some satisfaction in the flicker of displeasure that crossed his face at her use of his nickname. "After all we've been through the past few weeks, how could you think I would just accept you making a decision like this without talking to me first?"

He frowned. "This isn't about pride or holding out against the big bad wolf trying to buy your inn. I want you closer, where I know you're safe."

For a moment she faltered. He had gone about it in the most horrible manner possible. But was something else driving his actions? Was this all because he wanted to keep her and the baby safe? Protect them the way he felt like he hadn't protected his brother?

"And no matter how many pieces of furniture you replace, you can't run this place by yourself, especially once the child is born."

Her heart cracked. Had she thought that he had changed? Because he hadn't. He was still the same arrogant, conceited playboy used to getting his way.

"What do you propose I do then? Sell to you?"

"That's one option, yes."

"The preferable option," she shot back, anger filling her until she could barely speak without wanting to shout at him. She wouldn't tell him now that she had been considering doing just that. "Is that what all of this has been about? Your initial goal of buying my inn and fulfilling your whim of having property on Lake Bled for your precious hotel?"

"Don't," he warned as he leaned down and placed his hands on the arms of her chair, caging her in. "I didn't sleep with you so you'd sign away your property."

"No, you just slept with me because I was the next available woman." Furious, hurt that he could know so little about her, she pushed him away as she stood.

"You and I know there was much more to that night than just sex."

She crossed her arms, refused to look at him. "I don't know what I think anymore. I thought you knew me. I thought something more was developing between us."

Silence stretched between them, the awkwardness shifting into a painful, gut-wrenching stillness punctuated only by the occasional hiss of the logs in the fireplace. Had it been just a few weeks ago that they'd lain in front of another fire, his hand on her stomach, all of the beautiful possibilities of the future stretched out before them?

He ran his hand through his hair. "I told you before, Anika, there's only so much I can give you. I'm giving you everything I'm capable of."

"No, you're giving me everything you're willing to let yourself be capable of."

His eyes flashed. "I find it interesting that you judge me so harshly when you're not being honest with yourself."

"Excuse me?"

"You're working yourself into the ground. You're putting your health at risk, and our baby's, and for what? What do you want out of this place, Anika? Do you want to restore it to its former glory? How are you going to do that?"

His question hit her hard.

"Step by step," she finally replied.

"And why? So you can honor a family legacy? A legacy you told me you don't even really want to preserve?"

"If that's what you think, what you took away from what I shared with you," she said coldly, "then you don't know me at all."

"Oh, but I do." His tone was low, dangerous, as he advanced on her, his usual carefree expression dark, brows drawn together and eyes narrowed. "Pride. Not wanting to surrender control, to accept help."

"That's part of it," she admitted, taking a step closer to him. "But do you know why that pride matters so much? Because this is all I have left of my family. My mother grew up here. My *babica* was born here, married on the shores of the lake. If I give this up, I have nothing left."

As soon as the words left her lips, she wanted to snatch them back. Judging by the darkening expression on Nicholas's face, she'd gone too far.

"Nothing?" he repeated. "Not me, not our child?"

"The baby is my future. This place is my past, my present."

How could she make him understand how important this was? How much it meant to her to have this last connection to her family?

"You're holding on too tightly to the past, Anika."

"And what about you?" she countered.

"Me?"

"You act as if you've moved on. I appreciate everything you've done for the baby and me, Nicholas. But don't stand there and pretend like I'm the only one struggling with her past."

He glowered. "What am I not doing? I went to the ultrasound appointment with you, I've bought gifts for you and the baby, I showed up today when you needed me."

"All wonderful things, Nicholas. But when I ask you what we should name the baby, you pull away. When I ask if you think it's a boy or a girl, you change the subject. You do amazingly well at concrete things like buying things and reading articles. But you're keeping our child at arm's length."

"You know my history," he ground out. "I told you, I'm giving as much of myself as I can."

"But are you working on giving your all?" When he just stared at her, she plowed on. "I can be patient with you, Nicholas, just as you've been patient with me. But," she continued when he opened his lips to speak, "I can't move forward with my own personal development when you're essentially telling me that you'll never be able to fully commit to our child or me."

He stared at her for so long she wondered if he'd even heard what she'd said.

Then, finally: "And what if I can't? What if I can only offer you and the baby pieces of who I am?"

How was it possible for her to realize she was in love with the father of her child and have her heart smashed into a thousand pieces within the span of a few minutes?

She stared at Nicholas, her pulse beating so fast she could barely catch her breath. Her eyes caressed his handsome face, the hollows below his cheekbones, the straight slant of his nose, the faint stubble that had so entranced her the morning after they'd made love in Kauai.

She loved him so much. But loving someone didn't mean accepting less than what she deserved.

A cramping in her lower stomach interrupted her spiraling thoughts. Her breath caught as her fingers tightened on her belly.

Something's wrong.

Panic clawed up her throat.

"Nicholas..." She bit back a sob and reached out to him. He was by her side in an instant.

"What's wrong?" he demanded.

"The baby. Something's wrong with the baby."

CHAPTER FIFTEEN

NICHOLAS SAT BY the hospital bed, Anika's hand clasped in his. She'd fallen asleep sometime just before dawn.

The doctors had run a series of tests but found nothing wrong. The doctor had diagnosed the most likely scenario: normal muscle cramps exacerbated by stress.

Every moment in the hospital had made Nick remember the dark days when his brother had passed. The beeping of the machines, the distant sobs, the cold feeling deep in his belly. Every time a doctor came in, he'd tensed, fearing the worst news possible. He tried to maintain a brave face for Anika's sake. But as he sat there watching blood being drawn from her arm, watching her fingers fist the sheets at her sides as she waited for the next doctor to come in, all he could think was that once again he had caused someone pain.

And not just anyone. The mother of his child.

Tonight, when he had walked into the inn and seen her so pale, he'd been angry. Angry that while he had been off managing a ridiculous disagreement with one of the construction firms hired to work on the hotel in Greece, she had been working too hard, putting not only herself but the baby at risk. He'd been anxious to get back, to see her, to spend time with her.

Only to walk in and see her looking like death. He'd been scared, yes. Scared that she would work too hard, that something would go wrong. But he'd also felt guilty. He'd been sleeping on a brand-new bed on Egyptian cotton sheets while she'd been tucked away in that ramshackle building. One of the few things he could offer without reservations, or ties tethering him to the past, was his wealth. And he'd done nothing with it aside from a few token gifts.

When he said that she should move into the hotel with him, he had truly only been thinking of her. But her reaction to his proposal, her immediate jump to her initial accusations of the past, had brought out the worst in him.

Or had he merely lived up to her expectations, or lack thereof? He scrubbed his hand over his face. She had spoken the truth when she had accused him of not being able to fully commit.

He had tried. He had tried to open up the lock he kept on his heart, to let go of the fear.

He had failed.

As much as he had come to care for Anika, as many times as he had thought about what it would be like to hold the baby in his arms, he still could not allow himself to feel about her the way he was beginning to suspect she felt about him.

How cruel, he thought as he turned to look at her once more: the dark brush of her eyelashes against her pale skin, the slight curve to her mouth, the protective hand lying over her stomach. The sight of it sent a jolt of longing through him, but he quickly squashed it. Of course he would be feeling something in the moments after he had the terrifying scare of hearing her calling his name, asking for his help. Of seeing her eyes wild with panic, her teeth gritted in pain.

He hadn't known fear like that since the ambulance had sped away with David in the back. The day that his entire life had changed.

He had learned the hard way that people could act one way in the midst of a crisis and then, once it had passed, go back to being themselves or even become better versions of who they used to be. Sometimes, though, they became worse. Like his parents. After David's death, they had pulled together. Those first few months they'd been there for him, for each other.

But as the first anniversary of David's death had rolled around, something had changed. His mother had withdrawn from both of them, her depression taking her farther and farther away from her husband and only living son. His father had responded not by fighting for her, but by taking more and more trips to get away from the dark melancholy cloud hanging over their home. Leaving Nicholas to wallow in his own guilt.

When he talked with Anika at the castle, when he'd unburdened himself and she had done nothing but listen and accept him as he was, he'd felt cautious hope and a desire that went far deeper than just the physical for the incredible woman who just months ago had despised him. The way she had looked at him when he helped her with her porch repairs had made him feel more accomplished, more appreciated and more valued as a man than anything else he'd done to date.

And when they had made love that first night after the ultrasound, when he drifted his hand down to rest on her belly, he'd experienced the same sense of wonder he'd glimpsed on Anika's face when she'd seen the baby on the ultrasound screen. The time they'd spent together had drawn him further into the fantasy. Meals shared, walks taken, business ideas discussed, all with a woman he genuinely liked and was coming to care for. How much he'd missed her while in Greece had made him wonder if he could possibly change. If they could be more.

And then he'd walked into the inn and destroyed it all. Proven to himself and to her that he was not cut out for this. If he let things continue, allowed the relationship to go any further, he would just be hurting both of them. Marriage and family were never a part of his future. That he had felt anything beyond a simple liking and desire for Anika was an achievement in itself. But she wanted more.

No. She deserved more. So did their baby.

His chest clenched. The right thing for all of them was for him to let them go, even if the thought of someone else being with Anika, of being around his child made him want to throw something at the wall.

Wasn't the proof that he was emotionally incapable of being a father or a husband right in front of him? Once again, he had been so caught up in himself, in his own hurt, his own pride and confusion over Anika's obsession with the inn that he'd added to her stress. Even though the doctors had assured them that it was normal for women to experience dizziness and cramping in the first trimester, he still had not been able to shake loose the insidious guilt that he had caused her episode.

Anika started. Her eyes fluttered open and latched on to his face.

"Hey," she whispered softly.

"Hi," he replied, giving her hand a gentle squeeze.

"Have the doctors been back in yet?"

"No. But a nurse came by. The tests have continued to show everything as normal." He gave her hand another squeeze. "The baby's okay."

Tears pooled in her eyes and ripped open his chest.

"Thank you for coming. For bringing me here and staying."

"You don't need to thank me," he responded curtly.

She blinked and he inwardly cursed his sharp tone.

"I'm leaving." He sucked in a deep breath. "Once you're settled back at the inn, I have to take a trip to London."

A look of sadness passed across her face, one that gutted him. He wanted nothing more than to stay with her, to take her back to his hotel and tuck her into his bed, lie beside her all night.

"I won't be back for some time."

She frowned. "For how long?"

"At least a few months."

Her mouth dropped open. "Months?"

"I've been thinking about what you said." Slowly, he released her fingers and pulled back his hand. "You and the baby do deserve more. You deserve someone who can care about you more than I can, who can experience their emotions and not hold back. I'm not the kind of man who can commit to you that way."

He watched what little color was in her cheeks drain away.

"What are you saying?" she whispered.

"I still want to be involved in the child's life. But the majority of that involvement should be from a distance. I'm not good at getting emotionally involved. You told me your biggest dream was to have a family. The kind of family that you'd have with me wouldn't be the kind that made you happy. It would be one where you're constantly wondering if you're at fault, if there's somewhere else I'd rather be, if I'm actually going to stick around."

Her face twisted into something that looked far too much like pity.

"Is this about you," she asked gently, "or is this about your parents and what happened after your brother died?"

His body tensed. "A lot of it, yes. But it made me who I am today. I remember what it was like for those years after David died. How stilted everything was in the house. How I wondered if I was ever going to be enough, if we would ever be happy again." He ran a frustrated hand through his hair. "I'm not going to put you through that. I certainly will not put an innocent child through it just because I can't heal from my past."

Her lips parted. He stood before she could say anything else, before she could tempt him to stay, to put everything at risk once more and possibly fail.

"I've made my decision, Anika. I'll be in touch about financial arrangements and visitation."

She absently plucked at the hospital blanket draped over her legs. Slowly, she raised her gaze to his. Pain radiated from her eyes and stabbed straight into his heart.

"I understand."

It would be so much easier if she didn't understand. If she were like the other women in his life who would have been angry or frustrated or given him a big show of tears. But that wasn't Anika. It was one of the many things that he liked and appreciated about her—how much she cared for others, including him.

"In light of that, I agree this is for the best. And you're right." Her hand settled on her stomach. Regret washed through him that he hadn't touched her more, hadn't whispered to the tiny swell of her belly, hadn't had the guts to indulge her just once and talk about details like names and nursery colors. "The baby and I do both deserve someone who will be fully present, not just physically but emotionally." Her voice grew heavy. "I never thought I'd say this. But I wish it could have been you."

He hadn't thought he could hurt anymore. He'd been wrong. Grief dug its talons into his skin, clasped his heart and twisted. It was like David in some way, seeing her lie right in front of him yet just out of reach in this damned hospital bed. Yet it was different, worse, because this time he knew exactly who was to blame.

"I have really enjoyed getting to know you these past couple of months." Her small smile nearly killed him. "You're far much more than I gave you credit for."

"As are you, Anika. Our...the baby is lucky to have you as its mother." He swallowed past the tightness in his throat. "If you're comfortable, I would still appreciate seeing ultrasound photos. And a text every now and then. Knowing how you're doing."

She nodded once, the movement stilted.

He wasn't sure how long he stayed there, hands clenched at his sides, his gaze trained on her as if he was trying to memorize every detail of her face.

Finally, he turned and walked away.

CHAPTER SIXTEEN

NICHOLAS STARED DOWN at the paper in front of him. The contract he had been coveting for over a year finally signed on the dotted line.

There was no satisfaction; there was no excitement. There was only the hollow feeling that he had lost something far more precious than seeing his dream for the Hotel Lassard come to life.

His extended trip to London had lasted all of two weeks. He had arrived to evaluate one of the new properties going up on the north end of the city, only to find that a shortage of supplies had postponed the project indefinitely. He visited several other properties, staying for a day or two at a time. But all along he'd felt restless, a yearning to go back to the place that had started to feel like home.

He finally convinced himself that he was missing the shores of the lake: the distant Alps and the sight of the mystical castle standing guard over the town. Except when he had arrived and driven up the road leading to the hotel, he'd experienced nothing but a cold, bitter disappointment.

Home was no longer a place. Home had become a person, a woman he missed with every fiber of his being.

It would change, he kept telling himself. This was exactly what had happened to his parents, and to him, after David's death. Something in him would change. This sense of loss would lessen, leaving him a shell of what he needed to be to be the best person for Anika. The best father for their child.

For the most part he kept to the hotel, using the office to oversee the other properties. He booked a few visits to their resort in Dubai, the hotel in the Caribbean, the new resort going up on the peak of the Rocky Mountains in the middle of the United States. Everything he had been working for the past few years was coming to fruition.

Eventually it would satisfy him again. He just needed to get over this bump.

"Sir?"

Nicholas looked up to see his secretary standing in the doorway.

"Yes?"

"There's a woman here to see you."

Nicholas's heart hammered against his ribs. Slowly, he stood and walked to the door, keeping his pace as casual as possible.

"Darling!"

Nicholas's mother, Helen Lassard, walked to him, a wide smile on her face that dimmed when she took in his expression.

"I'm sorry, have I come at a bad time?"

He forced a smile onto his own face. "Not at all. I'm sorry, I've just had a lot on my mind. It's great to see you, Mother."

They hugged. She looked good, probably the best in nearly twenty years. The gauntness that had chiseled out her cheeks and made her look frail had disappeared. Her auburn hair was cut and colored to perfection, a classic bob around her heart-shaped face. A few more wrinkles here and there. But he was grateful to note the more noticeable ones were at the corners of her eyes and on the sides of her lips. "Smile lines," she had told him in the fall. There had been a time once when he had thought she might never smile again.

"Your father's been bragging about the Hotel Lassard at Lake Bled. I had to come and see your success for myself."

He took her on a tour of the hotel, showing her everything from the glamorous spa with its Roman bath–inspired grotto to the restaurant with its floor-to-ceiling windows that overlooked the lake. He took pride in her compliments, acknowledged the accomplishments that he had made with his latest hotel.

"And how goes your quest to secure the property next to the hotel?" she asked as they walked out the front door and into the coldness of a February morning. "The last time we spoke you wanted to add it as an expansion for the hotel. You were quite enthusiastic about it."

"I received the signed contract this morning."

He felt his mother's gaze on him.

"You don't sound too happy about that."

He shot her another forced smile.

"It's nothing. Just tired. The traveling I've been doing, the grand opening and now the addition of this contract, while very welcome, will mean longer hours trying to get everything prepared for next summer."

Whether she bought his excuse or not didn't really matter. He just wanted to get in the car and drive as far away as possible. On cold mornings like this, if he looked out the balcony doors of the penthouse to the west, he could see the weather vane on top of the inn's tallest turret poking above the branches.

He took his mother into Bled. They walked along Cesta Svobode, peeking into the various shops, pausing to grab lunch at a café alongside the lake.

"Oh, that castle," Helen said as the waiter brought him the check. "It looks so beautiful. Have you had a chance to tour it yet?"

"Once. The view is incredible."

"Do you have time to take your mother up there?"

He'd rather do anything but revisit the place where he'd first made himself vulnerable to Anika. Where their almost kiss had rekindled the passion that had been smoldering since Kauai and reawakened the desire she had stirred in him.

But he would have to get used to being in Bled, seeing the sites that he had experienced with Anika and not letting it ruin his day. He would also have to get used to the possibility of seeing Anika herself with their son or daughter, especially if she stayed here after the sale.

They drove up the winding road. Helen chatted on about the various things going on in London, his father's latest developments with the hotels that he managed, some of her old friends and everything that their children had accomplished.

"Linda's son recently got married," she said as they pulled up to the castle.

"Armand?" he said with some surprise. "I

never would have figured him for the type to get married."

"Neither would I," Helen said with a laugh. "But he's very happy. It's amazing what finding the right person can do to change how you might think about your future."

He slanted a glance at her. Had his father told her about Anika? Had they somehow found out about the baby? With the way that she was looking around at the scenery, her face serene, he doubted it. He'd always known that his mother had wanted grandchildren, had hoped that he might find a woman he could settle down with. If she had any inkling of what had been going on, she would have said something by now.

They toured the castle, coming out to stand on the same parapet where he had poured out his heart to Anika. He moved to the wall, his hand settling on the cold stone, his fingers scraping against the roughness. From this vantage point, he could see the inn perched on the edge of the lake.

"Is that it?" Helen asked as she came up to his side. "The property you just bought?"

He nodded once. Hard to believe that at one time buying the inn had been so important. Now the victory felt hollow.

"All right. Enough with the playacting."

He turned, surprised by the firmness in her voice.

"What?"

"I don't know. You tell me. Something's been bothering you since I arrived. You've never been one to mope, but it seems like you've just lost your best friend."

Nearly, he thought to himself. Anika had been everything he had ever wanted in a woman: kind, supportive, feisty, strong.

"I have lost someone," he finally said. "Someone that I care very deeply about."

His mother's eyes turned sad. She laid a gentle hand on his arm.

"Would you like to tell me what happened?"

He looked down at where her hand rested on his arm.

"It's not a happy story. I made a lot of mistakes. Too many," he murmured as he turned his gaze back to the inn.

"Not all stories are happy," Helen finally replied. "I've come to realize that over the years. That doesn't mean that they can't lead to joy later on."

He took a deep breath.

And then he told her everything. He told her about Anika, his quest to buy the inn. About his numerous run-ins with the spunky owner in the past year, culminating in their encounter in Hawaii, although he left out the more intimate parts. He started to tell her about Anika surprising him at the hotel and that his mother would have a grandchild before the first leaves of autumn fell. But something held him back. He didn't want that kind of news to be shared during such a dark confession.

Instead, he told her about how he and Anika had argued. How he'd hurt her.

"Did she want you to leave?"

Nicholas paused.

"I'm not sure what she wants," he said. "I don't know if she even knows herself. When we were in Hawaii, I saw another side of her. It was like the Anika that I saw here in Bled was muted, weighed down by all of her problems. But in Hawaii she…it was like watching her come alive."

A slow smile spread across Helen's face.

"You love her."

He stared at her. "What?"

"You love her."

Her words went round and round in his head, then settled in his heart with a brightness that he had never experienced.

"I do," he finally said. "I love her. But how can I possibly stay with her knowing I'll never be able to love her without restraint?"

Helen cocked her head. "What are you talking about?"

"I can't be the man that she needs me to be. After David…" His voice trailed off as pain spasmed across his mother's face. "Forget it. I shouldn't have brought this up."

"Don't." Helen held up a hand, took in a shuddering breath. "How many years did I not allow you to experience your own pain? How many years was I so focused on my own feelings that I failed you as a mother?"

Nicholas stared at her.

"That's what it is, isn't it?" she said softly. "You're worried that when something happens, she'll change or you'll change and things won't be the same. That there's the risk of going through what your father and I did. All those years apart, all those years of us being miserable."

Her words gave power to his deepest fears.

"Yes," he said. "We were happy before David died, and then for so many years…we weren't. Even now…"

"Your father and I are happy," Helen replied softly.

"Are you? Or is that just a line you trot out for your and others' benefit?"

He regretted the harsh words as soon as they left his mouth. But Helen didn't back down.

"We are. There are difficult times, yes. There always will be. You can't survive something like that without the grief popping up at random times and trying to pull you back under." She looked out over the idyllic tableau spread beneath them and sighed. "Those years after David's death weren't your fault, Nicholas. It was your father's and my fault. We should have gotten help far sooner than we did. That was our responsibility as your parents, as adults. It was something that we failed at. But it doesn't mean that if you and Anika were ever to experience a loss that's how you would handle it. Don't deny yourself a life with the woman you love because of my mistakes."

When she put it like that, it was hard to argue with her.

"What about your father and me?" Helen continued. "I know you love us, but what if something happens to us sooner than you expected? What about when something does happen? Are you going to keep us at a distance simply because of the possibility of what might happen?" Unshed tears glimmered in her eyes. "Please don't follow your father's and my mistakes. Learn from them and be better than we were. Be happy."

"When you phrase it like that," he admitted with a slight smile, "it does sound foolish. But

I'm not sure if I know how to open myself up to someone."

"I know." Helen sighed. "I suspected you kept your father and I at a distance, too. Not," she added as he started to speak, "that I blame you. I should have said something long ago. But I told myself I was analyzing too deeply, that you wouldn't call or visit as much as you did if there was a problem." Tears glinted in her eyes as she raised her chin up and looked at him. "I'm sorry, Nicholas. For all of it." Her hand came up and rested on his cheek. "But please don't let my mistakes take away the possibility of what you might have with this woman. It's foolish not to allow yourself to love her as much as I think you do."

"It is," he agreed. "But it's not just that." His gaze slid back to the inn. "I've already made so many mistakes. I don't know if she could trust me. It's always been about me telling her what I think is best, always me coming at it from the angle of either wanting to buy it or wanting to take it off her hands. Wanting to help make things better."

"I think you get that from what you experienced with your father and me. Even as a young boy, you always wanted to fix things. Admirable, if you go about it the right way. For me, I withdrew. For your father, it was easier to give you things, to take you on trips, than it was to deal with his depression."

His stomach rolled as he thought of what he had offered Anika: the money, the gifts…and the one thing that he hadn't. The one thing that Anika had asked for above all else, for him to open himself up to the possibility of truly loving their child.

"I'm not just saying this because I want to someday see you married and to give me grandchildren," Helen said with another smile.

Nicholas suppressed the quick surge of guilt at his mother's words. He would tell her eventually, but he wanted it to be a happy announcement, one that he could share with Anika by his side.

"From what little you've told me, son, she sounds like an amazing woman. One that you should be fighting for. I've never seen you this interested in anyone. For someone to do what she's done, to run an inn single-handedly by herself after so much loss, speaks volumes to her strength and character."

And it did, Nicholas realized with a surge of pride. He hadn't even taken the opportunity to fully admire what Anika had accomplished.

"I need to go to her. I need to fix this." Panic spurted inside him. "What if she doesn't accept my apology?"

"One step at a time. Yes, it might be hard for her. Whether she forgives or not is up to her. But," Helen added softly, "she sounds like a woman capable of such forgiveness. Give her the chance to choose."

Nicholas squared his shoulders. The inn gleamed like a jewel on the southern shores of the lake.

"I told her once that I don't lose." Determination hardened in his veins. "I certainly don't intend to start now."

CHAPTER SEVENTEEN

ANIKA WALKED THROUGH the lobby of the inn, smiling at a couple of the guests clustered by the roaring fireplace. Lori, one of her new hires, walked by with a tray of tea and biscuits.

Everything was running smoothly. Anika hadn't yet told the staff about the pending sale to the Hotel Lassard. She would eventually, and hoped that her requirement that the hotel retain all of her staff while providing them with a generous pay raise would soothe any concern they might have.

It was funny, she thought as she walked to the tiny little nook at the back of the kitchen that overlooked the lake, she had expected to feel sadder about finally signing her name on the contract. Instead, all she had felt was relief. There would be some sadness. She would miss things like arranging excursions for the guests, growing the inn the way Marija and she had dreamt about. But she wouldn't miss the day-to-day operations, like having to get up in the middle of the night if a guest needed her or reviewing the books and making sure all of the accounts balanced.

A yawn escaped. She was exhausted, but every time she closed her eyes at night and tried to fall back asleep, her mind raced. She had hurt Nicholas. All because she didn't want him to hurt her first. Because she was scared of falling deeper in love with him when he continued to hold back. Because she hadn't been patient enough to give him time. Perhaps they would have realized that they weren't meant to be together. But perhaps, with more time and patience on her part, it could have been something beautiful.

Her eyes drifted back toward the trees that separated the Hotel Lassard from the Zvonček Inn. Should she reach out to him? Give him space? Or accept that, whether or not she was open to trying a little longer, he was done?

The thought tightened her throat and she turned away. If that were the case, she would do what she always did—adapt and move forward. Perhaps she and the baby could go somewhere else where she could take on a role that combined the things she loved. Maybe a job in marketing or excursions, with fewer demands on her schedule allowing her to be fully present as a mother. That and, as the baby grew, time to travel, to share adventures with her little one.

All thoughts for another time, she decided. For now, she would focus on waiting to hear back from the Hotel Lassard's lawyers. She had sent the contract through the business channels, even though part of her had wanted to reach out to Nicholas to explain why she had finally decided to sign.

As painful as it had been, her conversation with Nicholas had opened her eyes to how she was hanging on to something that needed to be let go. The inn was not her family. Yes, it represented a rich history, and yes, it had been Marija's dream. But it wasn't hers, and Marija had always been nothing if not supportive of Anika going after her own dreams. Keeping herself tethered to the inn out of a sense of loyalty was not what her *babica* would have wanted, and certainly not the right fit for Anika or her child.

Letting go of her pride and placing the inn in the hands of someone she trusted to do it justice was the hardest thing she had done to date. But it was the right thing.

Suddenly restless, she slipped on her red boots and gray coat and slipped out the back door. Snow crunched underfoot as she drew closer to the dock. Steam drifted up from the water, creating a hazy, magical mist. Brilliant sunshine, so bright it almost hurt, made the world glow white. In the distance, the church spire stood proudly against the sky.

Her pulse beat in her throat, each hard thump making it harder to hold back her tears. A week before the grand opening, Nicholas had suggested going out to the island. But she'd already scheduled the handyman for more work on the inn, including some projects she'd needed to walk him through.

Next time, she had promised.

She tilted her head back and looked up at the brilliant blue sky. What could they have been if she had asked him to stay in the hospital room? What could they have been, not just as parents, but as a couple, as partners, if he could let go of his past and she could have not been so damned stubborn?

A crunch sounded behind her. Irritated that a guest was intruding on her grieving, she swiped a hand at her cheek in case any wayward tears had escaped and turned around.

Her heart stopped. Nicholas stood in front of her, mere steps away, dressed in black pants and a black winter coat, the red scarf he'd worn the day he'd helped her with the porch wrapped around his neck. The black reminded her of what he'd worn that fateful night in Kauai when they'd danced on the patio with the wild ocean roaring just beyond the cliffs. She'd thought him a demon then, or perhaps even the devil.

But now, as she looked at the handsome face that had become so familiar to her, and felt the pain in his eyes as if it were her own, he reminded her more of a fallen angel.

"Sorcha."

She blinked. Of all the things she had expected him to say, that was not it.

"Sorcha?" she repeated.

He took a step closer, his movements slow, as if he were afraid she'd run away at the slightest provocation.

"It means 'bright' or 'radiant.' Scottish, although it's used in Ireland, too."

The tiniest flame of hope flickered to life in her chest.

"I'd have to think about it. But I like it."

"And Geoffrey if it's a boy," he said as he moved closer still. "Geoffrey David Lassard."

She swallowed hard. "Now, that one I don't have to think about. It's perfect."

Slowly, he reached up, cupping her face the way he had in the hotel hallway, with such tenderness it made her want to weep.

"I've barely been able to sleep," he whispered. "All I can think about is you. You and…" His other hand came up, paused, then rested on her belly. "Our child." He leaned down, rested his forehead against hers. "Anika, I've been such a fool."

She rose up on her toes and flung her arms around his neck. His arms came around her, crushing her to his body before he loosened her.

"The baby—"

"Is just fine. Don't let go, Nicholas. Please don't let go."

He threaded his gloved fingers through her hair, pulled her head back and crushed his lips to hers. She returned his kiss with every ounce of passion and love she had.

"I missed you," she whispered between kisses.

"And I you." He lifted his head but kept her enclosed in his embrace. "I'm terrified, Anika. I told myself in the beginning that I needed to go all in if I was going to be involved in raising our child. But every time I tried to let myself experience the joy I saw on your face that day you had the ultrasound, it was like there was a wall I couldn't get past. I told myself it was because I wasn't capable. But it wasn't." He let out a harsh breath. "It was fear. Fear and years of unresolved resentment and anger toward my parents."

Her heart broke for him. She had suffered loss, too, but she had never doubted that her parents or her *babica* had loved her.

"That's on them, Nicholas. Not you."

He smiled slightly. "My mother told me the same thing."

"Your mother?"

"She came to visit. We had the first truly honest conversation about David's death and what happened in the years after that." His fingers traced a pattern on her cheek, his eyes never leaving hers. "She told me that fear of what might happen in the future was a poor reason to hold oneself back. That whenever she thought of that time after David's passing, she would always mourn, but she would never regret the work she put into getting better, nor the life she's found after loss."

Anika reached up and brushed his hair back from his forehead. "How do you feel about that?"

"Good. Sad, but good. It'll take a while for my parents and me to fully repair that relationship. I had always thought I had been the most successful one to move on from David's death. But I did the same thing they did, losing myself in school and sports, then university and work."

"You were a child yourself," she reminded him with a little heat in her voice. "You shouldn't have been left to deal with that on your own."

"No. My parents made mistakes. But as an adult, I have the choice to do things differently now. Starting with an apology. I'm sorry I walked away from you, Anika, and our child. I'm sorry I pushed to get what I wanted, to not truly listen to your reasons for wanting to hold on to the inn."

She smiled through her tears. "But you were right, you know. I was holding on to it for the wrong reasons. We were both holding on to the past. It was safer to focus on the inn and the connection I already had than risk forging a new one. I was so focused on what I might lose by selling the inn that I couldn't see all the wonderful possibilities in front of me. Although," she added, "it was very satisfying in the beginning telling you no."

He smiled. "I hope you'll have a different answer for my next question."

Her breath caught as he dropped to one knee in the snow. He reached into his coat pocket and brought out a small black box, opening it to reveal a beautiful ring with delicate strands of silver winding over the most incredible sapphire she'd ever seen.

"I love you, Anika. I never thought I'd be capable of loving someone the way I love you. And I can't promise there won't be days I still question whether I'm capable or not, whether or not I'm doing things right. But I can promise that I won't give up and I won't stop trying to be the kind of man you and our child deserve."

Tears streamed down her cheeks as she looked down into the face of the man she loved.

"Yes." She barely choked the word out as he slid her glove off and put the ring on her finger.

"I picked the sapphire because it reminded me of the way the ocean looked in Hawaii." He stood, looking down at the ring as his hand curled around hers. "How blue it was when you jumped off the pier looking like a mermaid. How it felt when you reached out and grabbed my hand while we were snorkeling. How untamed it looked when we watched the storm from the balcony." His eyes came up to capture hers, the heat and passion stealing her breath. "I knew I wanted you before we went to Hawaii. I wanted you like I'd wanted nothing else before. But it was the moment you held my hand under the waves, and then when you smiled like you had just seen the most spectacular thing in the world, that I started to fall in love with you."

"Funny," she said as she reached up and laid her bare hand on his cheek, the ring glinting in the sunlight, "it wasn't too long after that I started to fall in love with you. The night of the gala, when we danced, when you called to check on me, when we sat and talked in the dark…" She leaned up on her toes and brushed her lips against his. "I realized how much more there was to you than fancy suits and smug smiles. And you saw me," she murmured against his mouth. "You saw me and told me how special I was, and I felt myself fall right then and there."

He kissed her again before he leaned back and pulled an envelope out of his pocket. She took it, frowning at the unexpected weight.

"I was hoping I could offer this to you as a wedding present." She opened it, pulling out little square cards with different paint colors on them. "Instead of the Hotel Lassard purchasing the inn, I'd like to help you renovate it. Bring it back to its former glory."

Tears fell again, making the envelope crinkle as they hit the paper.

"Nicholas…"

"I should have offered this to you a long time ago." He brushed a hand over her hair. "I was so focused on my dream that I disregarded yours."

"And I appreciate that. More than I can express." She ran her fingers over the paint colors, indulged in a brief fantasy of what it would be like to see the inn with a fresh coat of paint, a new roof, a renovated front porch. Savored the image.

Then let it go.

"But I'm no longer the right person to run it. My heart isn't in it. I want to travel and, most importantly, I want to be there for you and our baby." She glanced over his shoulder at the inn. There was grief in letting go, but also a hint of excitement. It would be a fresh start for all of them, a chance to truly move on. "After seeing how you run your hotels, knowing the reason behind why you do what you do, I knew signing the contract was the right thing to do."

He turned and together they studied the inn.

"I had planned on making Bled my home base, at least for a few years," Nicholas finally said. "Would you be comfortable living here in Bled and traveling with me for work?"

Anika smiled. "Yes. That was always one of the things I struggled with. I had my mother's wanderlust, but Babica's love of having a home to come back to. And," she added as she looked back over her shoulder at the town perched on the north shore, "Bled has been my home for so long. Knowing we'll always be able to come home will make the adventures that much more enjoyable."

"Then I would appreciate having you play a part in the renovation of the inn, ensuring that the vision of the Hotel Lassard brand blends with the legacy of your family."

Her heart swelled. "Thank you."

He turned her in the circle of his arms. "And

at least a couple of stays every year, for quality control."

"Of course."

His smile faded as he looked down at her with a serious expression. "I love you, Anika. I'm not sure what the next few months are going to be like. But I do know I don't want to be anywhere but with you."

She cupped his face in her hands and rose up on her toes.

"I love you, Nicholas. And I know it's not going to be perfect. But," she said just before she kissed him, "I have a feeling it's going to be our best adventure."

EPILOGUE

THE ORANGE AND red leaves glowed beneath the rays of the autumn sun as the gondola pulled up to the dock. Nicholas stepped out onto the wooden boards and turned, his breath catching at the sight of the woman still seated in the boat.

"Are you ready, Mrs. Lassard?"

Anika smiled up at him. Her dark hair fell in loose curls past her shoulders. The ivory gown she'd selected for their intimate wedding at the castle bared her shoulders, adding a hint of sexiness to an otherwise elegant dress that clung to her body all the way down to her knees before flaring out into a cascade of silken folds.

He held out a hand, hot possessive need flowing through him at the sight of the silver band on her finger. An hour ago, they'd exchanged vows in the upper courtyard of Bled Castle with his parents and a couple of close friends in attendance.

And their daughter. *His* daughter, who had

watched over the ceremony in a little white dress that brought out the golden brown of her eyes and a gummy smile.

When he looked back over the transition he'd undergone in the past year, it amazed even him how starkly things had changed. He'd offered to purchase the inn and have it made into a home. But Anika had stayed firm: she wanted the inn renovated to be enjoyed by guests. Zvonček House, a Hotel Lassard property, would open in the spring and was already booked a year out.

As they'd balanced traveling in her second trimester for his work and overseeing the renovations, they'd stumbled across a home tucked away in the mountains with a two-story living room, massive windows that provided a jaw-dropping view of the lake and acres for their little one to run around on. The words "I love it" had barely escaped Anika's mouth before he'd told his realtor to make the deal.

The painters had just finished painting the nursery adjoining their bedroom a pale lavender when Anika had gone into labor four weeks early. When he'd first held Sorcha Lassard in his arms, his wonder had been offset by a resurgence of his old fear. She'd been so tiny, so dependent on him and Anika for everything, that it had been a struggle to stay present and not give in. It hadn't been easy, but he'd kept his vow to Anika and their child. From rocking a wailing Sorcha at midnight to learning how to change diapers and bathe a tiny infant, he'd tackled every task he could to be there for his daughter and help Anika.

It had been after one of those baths just a couple weeks ago that he'd lifted Sorcha out of the little baby tub, wrapped her in a tiny towel and watched a smile bloom across her face as she looked up at him.

And just like that, he'd experienced the same wonder he'd seen on Anika's face at the ultrasound appointment. He'd hollered for his wife, begged Sorcha to do it again and laughed when she'd proven to have both her parents' stubborn streak and refused to smile for another three days.

And his wife—*his wife*, he thought with masculine pride—had given him the time to get there, supporting and loving him through the highs and lows of those first tumultuous weeks of parenthood.

"Are you sure you can do this?" Anika asked as she joined him on the dock, casting a skeptical glance at the stone steps that climbed up the hillside of the island.

"I'll try not to take that as an insult."

She laughed. "But it's ninety-nine steps! I

don't think I could even walk that without needing to rest."

He pulled her against him, savored her sharp
intake of breath as their bodies collided. He
would never tire of this rush, this desire mixed
with the intimacy of loving someone as he loved
Anika.

"Trust me?"

"Always."

"Well, then, Mrs. Lassard…" He leaned down
and scooped her up. A laugh followed her initial squeal of surprise as her arms flew around
his neck. "Onward and upward."

He carried her up the entire flight, kissing her
soundly at the top before setting her on her feet.
They walked into the church hand in hand. The
chapel, complete with wooden pews and gold-
framed paintings on the white walls, was small
but beautiful. While Nicholas had included it
in his recommendations for guests at Anika's
suggestion, waiting until now to actually experience it himself had been worth it.

Anika approached the rope hanging from the
ceiling. It connected to the wishing bell she had
spoken about the first time they'd had lunch
after she'd told him about the baby. She smiled
at him.

"Ready?"

"I am."

They grasped the rope and pulled once, twice, three times. The bell tolled, a rich sound that echoed off the arching ceiling. Anika looked up, her eyes crinkling as she laughed.

"This is incredible." She looked at him then with such love shining from her eyes it nearly knocked him off his feet. "Thank you."

He moved to her side and swept her up into his arms.

"You don't have to carry me back down the stairs," she said with another laugh as he carried her out of the chapel. "The legend says you just had to make it to the top."

"I know." He grinned at her. "But I don't want to let you go."

She shook her head even as a blush stole over her cheeks. "I can see why all the women fell for your charm, Mr. Lassard."

"You're the only one who matters, Mrs. Lassard."

He carried her out into the sunshine and back down the steps. By the time they reached the bottom, the gondola carrying his parents and Sorcha had arrived. His father cradled Sorcha in his arms, pointing out various sights around the lake, while his mother looked on with happiness radiating from her eyes.

"Did you make it up?" Helen asked.

"He did," Anika said as she kissed his cheek.

"Impressive, son." Henry grinned at him with a teasing glint in his eyes. "Didn't know you had it in you."

It was amazing, Nicholas thought as he took his daughter in his arms and kissed her forehead, how quickly he and his parents had healed. After learning they were gaining not only a daughter-in-law but a grandchild, they had made frequent trips to Bled over the last few months. Trips that had included long talks, tears and apologies.

There was still work to be done. But Nicholas could honestly say it was the first time in over two decades that all three of them were truly happy.

Sorcha curled into the protective curve of his arm, her eyes fixated on his face. Her tiny lips tilted up and his chest grew warm.

"We have the *pletna* for another hour," Henry said. "Then it will take us back to the castle."

"With plenty of time to rest and refresh before the reception," Helen added.

"Then go and enjoy the island," Anika urged. "I've never been to a two-hundred-guest wedding reception before, but I imagine we're all going to be very busy tonight."

Henry and Helen walked up the stairs hand in hand, and Nicholas cradled Sorcha on his shoulder as he tugged Anika closer.

"Do we have to go to the reception?" he whispered, savoring the way she shivered as he gently kissed her on the neck.

"It is *our* reception."

His hand drifted up and down her back, the heat of her skin seeping through the thin material.

"But if we left early we could—"

"Little ears!" Anika said as she cut him off with a laugh.

"All right. But you owe me at least one dance."

"You know what, I like you so much I'll give you two." She kissed one of Sorcha's chubby cheeks before she looped her arms around Nicholas's waist. "So, what did you wish for?"

"If I tell you, doesn't that mean it won't come true?"

She wrinkled her nose. "I suppose that's true."

"I can make an exception, then, because I didn't make a wish."

A frown crossed her face. "You didn't?"

"No. Because," he said, just before he kissed his wife, "you already made my wish come true."

* * * * *

Couldn't get enough of
An Heir Made in Hawaii?
*Then you'll love exploring these other
pulse-racing reads by Emmy Grayson!*

A Deal for the Tycoon's Diamonds
A Cinderella for the Prince's Revenge
The Prince's Pregnant Secretary
Cinderella Hired for His Revenge
His Assistant's New York Awakening

Available now!